HEAVEN'S DOOR

Tom Doughty

First Stillwater River Publications Edition
Library of Congress Control Number: 2021903621
Paperback ISBN: 978-1-952521-88-1
1 2 3 4 5 6 7 8 9 10
Written by Tom Doughty.
Published by Stillwater River Publications,
Pawtucket, RI, USA.
**Publisher's Cataloging-In-Publication Data
(Prepared by The Donohue Group, Inc.)**

Names: Doughty, Tom, 1949- author.
Title: Heaven's door / Tom Doughty.
Description: First Stillwater River Publications edition. | Paw-
tucket, RI, USA : Stillwater River Publications, [2021]
Identifiers: ISBN 9781952521881
Subjects: LCSH: United States. Air Force--Airmen--Fiction. |
Coups d'état--Greece--Athens--Fiction. | Hostages--
Greece--Athens--Fiction. | Air bases--Greece--Athens--
Fiction.
Classification: LCC PS3604.O9251 H43 2021 | DDC 813/.6--
dc23
*The views and opinions expressed in this book
are solely those of the author
and do not necessarily reflect the
views and opinions of the publisher.*

Table of Contents

ARRIVAL
ATHENAI AIRBASE
1971

Claudius Boatman stood before the Athenai Air Base police station as he held out a flat palm overflowing with unfamiliar Greek coins. He had been in-country for five minutes, noticed how hot it was, noticed the tamarind trees lining Main Base Road, and allowed the taxi driver his pick of the coins. As the driver was choosing his fee, a round, short, hairy, red-headed, red-skinned sergeant, looking fierce and angry, marched out of the office. The sergeant had seen this scene a dozen times before and without thought retrieved half of the coins from the driver, gave them back to Claudius, and sent the driver on his way. He said, "These are called drachmas, thirty to the dollar. Follow me."

Claudius shouldered his green duffle bag, the only thing to distinguish him as military since he wore civilian clothes, and entered the station. The redhead waited for him inside. Claudius saw from his name tag that his last name was Whittle. The redhead asked, "Who are you?"

The five stripes on Whittle's shoulder told Claudius that he was a tech sergeant, so his own replies could be informal; he need not tack a "sir" at the ends of his sentences. He answered, "Airman First Class Claudius Boatman. You should be expecting me."

"Well, Airman First Class Claudius Boatman, we're not expecting you, but since you're already here, you might as well sign in. Had you known, you might have gotten away with taking a couple of days off, but now it's too late. You know that this is a two-and-a-half-year tour, three if you extend?"

"Three years? Stateside they told me it was an eighteen-month tour."

"Sure they did, and I bet you were told that you wouldn't be humping airplanes."

"That's right."

"You were also told that you'd be working at either the Embassy or the civilian airport, trying to pick up hammers all day."

"That's right."

"Did you see those C-130s on the way in?"

"The cargo planes? Yeah, I saw them."

"You'll be humping them tomorrow. You have one day to in-process. Tomorrow, you come back here at 1900 hours. We're in a recall. We're working twelve hours on, twelve off. Arab terrorists have threatened to blow up the base for the umpteenth time, so we're on alert. Welcome to Greece."

"Thanks."

"By the way, what's your nickname?"

"I don't have a nickname."

"Everybody's got a nickname."

"At my last base, they called me Liberty, like Liberty Valance."

"Liberty, huh, like the song?"

"Yeah, what's yours?"

"I don't have one." There was an implied challenge in Whittle's denial. He had set out to fool Liberty and he had succeeded.

Claudius said, "I bet your nickname is Red. I once had a dog named Red. He used to try to screw my leg all the time."

"Oh, so you're a smart-ass. We don't like smart-asses around here."

The two men looked into one another's hard eyes as each considered the next course of action. Whittle took a step forward and Liberty fought the instinct to step back. He continued to meet Whittle's glare. The sergeant asked, "You got your orders?"

"What orders?"

"The orders that sent you here."

"Yeah, I got them."

"Well, where are they?"

"In my bag."

"Are you going to get them?"

"Yeah, I'll get them."

Liberty reached down for his bag, half expecting an "accidental" bump from Whittle to make him fall. When nothing happened, the tension snapped, and the two men relaxed. Liberty handed Whittle his orders. While the tech sergeant perused them, Liberty had a chance to look about the station. The room they were in was small and gray, holding a gray metal desk behind which sat a couple of empty, gray metal folding chairs. The walls were painted gray and the door through which they passed was a thick, gray metal door. Liberty could see into the remaining two rooms of the station. Both were as tiny as the room in which he stood. The closest room was cut in half by a paneled partition that had a door and a window on one side. This was the desk sergeant's office. The door was always locked, and the desk sergeant was peeking through the window. The room farthest away held the jail. The building had no outside windows. Liberty said, "You have a nice place here."

"We try. It says here that you're supposed to work as a security guard at the radio shack. You want law enforcement, right?"

"I don't know. I've never worked law enforcement. I didn't go to tech school for that."

"Good. We'll put you into law enforcement." Whittle yelled, making Liberty start, "Tyler, get out here!"

From the desk sergeant's office emerged a tall, strong Black man with caramel-colored skin. His features were handsomely sharp and his body well-muscled. Whittle said, "Tyler, this is Claudius Boatman. He'll be working with us for a while. Drop him off at the barracks. You might want to give him a tour of the base first."

Tyler asked, "The whole square mile?"

"If you have the time. Boatman, come back in a couple of hours, after you've had time to settle in a little, and we'll start you in-processing."

Liberty gave Whittle a mock salute, flipping his hand out like a British soldier, while lifting his right leg, forcefully slamming his foot down, and loudly calling, "Aye-aye, Sarge."

Whittle addressed the desk sergeant, not caring that Liberty heard him, "Hey, Hawk, you're gonna really like the new guy, a real jerk if there ever was one!"

Once outside, Liberty stopped in front of a row of blue cars and pickup trucks. He asked Tyler, "Which one?"

"The pickup nearest you."

Liberty threw his bag into its bed and got into the cab with his escort. As he drove down base, Tyler said, "Speed limit on base is fifteen miles per hour. The building on our left is the Office of Special Investigations, OSI, the local spies. This is obviously a ball field. To the left again is the post office. Opposite it are the bowling alley and the BX. You'll get to know the bowling alley well because of all the drunks. Here's the barracks, but we have only half a mile more to go. That building over there is personnel. You'll have to drop in there within the next couple of hours. Over there is The Crossroads. That's the cafeteria where everyone hangs out. That's where you pick up the dependent girls. OOOOOO! There's one now! Look at that ass! OOOOOO! God! Is she gorgeous!"

Tyler slowed his vehicle to five miles per hour. The girl he was referring to was a seventeen-year-old dependent, long hair, lithe body, fine face, and waiting to cross the road. She wore jeans which couldn't have been tighter and a halter top that accentuated her budding breasts. Tyler pulled up next to her. "Hey, Tammy, how ya doin'?"

She smiled. "Fine."

"This here's Claudius Boatman. He likes you."

She laughed. "Hi, Claudius Boatman, where are you from?"

Liberty had been asked this several times in his military career and gave the answer he found most appropriate. "Rhode Island, near Boston."

Tammy leaned into the window on Liberty's side. She said, "I'm from Virginia, near West Virginia." Their eyes twinkled. Tammy said, "I got to go. See you later."

Liberty said, "Yeah, later."

Tyler said, "Bye, Tammy," and when she was out of earshot, he added, "You can poon her if you want."

"Yeah, I know."

Tyler resumed his driving. "She's only seventeen, but she looks great, doesn't she?"

"I'll say."

"I think it's the hot climate here. They ripen early and they're hot. Last year she disappeared for a couple of weeks. They found her shacking up with a Navy guy. It's not too unusual here. A lot of girls take off for weeks at a time, then come back to mom and dad when they're tired of doing whatever they're doing."

"What happened to the squid? I mean, he *did* commit statutory rape."

"Nothing. That building to our left is the hospital. Check out this building on our right. That's the laundromat. That's where you go to pick up the young wives."

"Is there a lot of cheating here?"

"All the wives cheat and I know this from personal experience. About half the husbands cheat. There's the library, not a bad one for such a small base. They even have books on nuclear physics in there." Tyler came to a full stop at the end of Main Base Road. They were sitting before one of the largest buildings on base, somewhat the size of a large bookstore. "This is Base Ops. There's a snack bar here. On the other side is the flight line where the C-130s are parked. We share our runway with the civilian airport and the Greek airbase. That's where you'll be once you're in-processed. Try to get the nightshift."

"I'm supposed to report tomorrow night."

"Then you're in luck. The dayshift guys cook their agates off; you could literally cook an egg on the truck's hood, but it's not so bad at night. On the way back, I'll show you the base commander's office."

After doing so, Tyler pulled up before another large gray building. He said, "This is the police barracks. The First Sergeant's office is on the near end. I'll catch you later."

"Okay, thanks for the lift." Liberty retrieved his duffle bag and stood looking at the long, rectangular, gray building that would be his home for a long, long time. His eyes had a flat, deadened expression as they scanned his surroundings like radar impassively scanning a hostile sky.

Hell is supposed to be hot and glaring and here, beneath the Greek sun, it was certainly hot and glaring, so much so that Liberty, who had yet to develop the habit of wearing sunglasses, squinted for the brightness of the day. Hell is supposed to be a land of lies and he had certainly been lied to. Hell is supposed to be a land of no hope. What future did he have here? He failed college and he failed his family. Although he was told not to take the Vietnam War and the war protests personally, he felt that America wanted him, and strong men like him, dead. America hated him because of its own weaknesses and desires. He did take the war personally since he was the one meant to die. Someone screwed up sending him to Greece.

He looked at the tamarind trees lining the parking lot of the barracks. The lawn in front of the barracks was the only green he'd seen since his arrival. During the landing, he had seen sand, bare rock, stunted trees, and the square, white buildings of Athens.

He remembered his favorite quote from *Paradise Lost*: "What though the field be lost? All is not lost – th' unconquerable will, and study of revenge, immortal hate, and courage never to submit or yield." Inwardly, he smiled, although outwardly only the line of his mouth lengthened. It was a good thing that Professor Williston, himself a misfit, had him memorize those lines.

As he stood there, the sun seemed suddenly oppressive and overbearing and ruined the narcotic effect of the tamarind trees. His duffle bag grew heavy and strained the muscles of his right shoulder. As he was shifting the bag from his right to his left shoulder, a tall, thin man with scraggly blond hair walked by him. He wore cut-off jeans, a tee-shirt, sandals, and granny sunglasses. As the man passed, he said, "Hey, pig! What are *you* doing here? Go back to the pigsty you escaped from!"

Immediately, Liberty swung around to face his accuser. He was enraged and wanted to fight. He slipped the bag from his shoulder and was about to chase the quickly retreating figure, when it occurred to him that he'd have to leave his bag behind and take a chance of losing, literally, everything he owned. He decided not to give chase. He'd remember that face, though, and get him later at his own convenience. It was only a matter of time.

He carried his bag into the First Sergeant's office, where he was greeted by a pleasant Black man, all teeth and eyeglasses. It suddenly occurred to him that he'd seen a disproportionate number of Black men on base, which, since Greece was considered a good duty assignment, belied the media's assertion that all Blacks got the worst jobs in the worst places.

The Firstie had Liberty sign in and brought him to his room. He said, "We try to limit our space to one man per room despite the fact that each room has three bunks in it. When we start doubling up, we take the first batch of men and give them an allotment to live off-base. It's a good deal. A house, a whole house, rents here for ninety dollars a month and off-base housing is one hundred and fifty a month. You make out like a bandit. I'll put you on the waiting list."

"Thanks, Sarge."

Liberty unpacked and put his gear into the gray wooden lockers that lined one side of his room. He had a gray metal desk, a gray metal chair, a large yellow comfort chair, and a large brown wooden bureau. Later, he would get a refrigerator when some senators, who wanted to sightsee and play tennis, decided to "inspect" the base.

Liberty was hungry and went to The Crossroads, a perfectly flat, squat building. Upon his entrance, he noticed the gray metal dining tables surrounded by fluorescent-orange plastic chairs in a poor attempt at modernization. On one side of the large dining area was the bookstore sporting the *Stars and Stripes* and a fairly good collection of paperback books. On the other side of the room was the grill where Liberty stood in line to order his steak.

Unlike the other Greeks he'd seen so far, the cook was fair with red hair, whereas the other Greeks had all been dark with black hair. The cook had a bad cold and he let his nose drip instead of wiping it off. The clear fluid dropped onto the grill in little puffs and hisses. Liberty watched carefully to see if any fell on his steak, but none seemed to land there. He was surprised that no one in the line said anything.

As he moved his tray along the rail, he ordered corn and potatoes from the Greek women serving the dishes. He paid in U.S. dollars and was again surprised to see that the Greek at the register had no fingers, using the stubs of his fingers to punch the register keys. Liberty was later to learn, as rumor had it, that the man's fingers were cut off in New York City by thieves in a hurry to get his gold rings.

As he was eating, Liberty watched the social dynamics of the cafeteria. There were 500 GIs stationed here as well as 1,500 dependents. That meant that he would get to know everyone on base, at least by face. Two groups dominated the cafeteria: teenagers between the ages of 15 and 18, and the young GIs and their wives who were in their early twenties. Although there was some crossing of unspoken barriers, the two groups, generally, stayed to themselves.

Libido was everywhere. It was obvious how the teenaged girls, proud of their physical development and knowing how the unmarried GIs hungered for them, flaunted themselves, making sure their breasts jutted out to advantage, wearing loose tee-shirts so they could bend over to expose their breasts while making it look like an accident, and always walking in a saucy way to accentuate their figures caught in jeans two sizes too small.

The young wives were also a part of the libido quest, except that they were more cunning. As he was eating his meal, Liberty noticed a particularly good-looking woman sitting between two airmen. She wore a wedding ring and was, presumably, married to one of the men. Casually, she glanced at Liberty and just as casually shifted in her seat so that she faced him. While she talked with the two men, she opened her legs ever so slightly, then a little wider, and with every move she looked at Liberty to make sure he was watching. Even though she wore slacks, Liberty found her mannerisms provocative. When she stood to leave her table, she ran a hand along her outer thigh and gave Liberty a profile view of her body. Then she threw him a sharp, penetrating glance that almost made him drop his fork. He thought, *she wants to know*.

Liberty ate his meal as though he was waging war. First, he ate his corn. When that was annihilated, he attacked his potatoes and finished them off. The final assault was made on the steak. At his first bite he retched. The taste was strong and brought to his mind images of garbage cans and maggots rotting in a hot sun. He was so hungry, though, that he forced it down. It was the first time he had ever eaten unprocessed, aged meat.

He had been saving the last inch of his soda to wash it down and to get rid of the dusty, dry feeling in his throat, but just as he reached for it, a Greek busboy snatched it away so quickly and efficiently that Liberty didn't have time to react. It was then that he noticed how the busboys did this to everyone not quick enough to grab his drink the moment a white blazer made a pass at the table. Liberty watched a dozen attempts fail as a muscular, tanned arm reached adroitly up, caught the cup as it was disappearing, and saved the soda. Frequently, though, the busboys met with success. It was an undeclared game, and no one got angry.

Liberty mused at the odd quirk of fate that had brought him here. When he volunteered for Greece, he was told that he had a one in a million chance of being sent there. By distance, he was a third of the way around the world from his native Rhode Island. By culture, from the brief glimpse he'd had so far, he seemed to be thirty years in the past. The Greeks dressed in dark, heavy clothing, drove old, dusty cars, and the men still hoped to marry virgins.

Liberty returned to his room, closed and locked his door, and immediately felt protected. Once he closed that door, the world ceased to exist. Vietnam, war protests, Rhodesia, guard duty, Arab terrorists, minority rights, pollution, death, agony, all ended as soon as he closed out the world. Here, he could be alone. He only had to close his door and not answer it should anyone come looking for him. Here, he could read and study his correspondence courses and get lost in a world of thought. He could even escape the failures and weaknesses that drove him to enlist.

Liberty opened his locker and scanned the ten books that he had brought with him. He decided to read "Self-Reliance" from a collection of Emerson's essays. The next couple of hours would be a true pleasure for him. *Then,* he thought, *I'll in-process.*

The next day, Liberty arrived at the police station an hour early. Guard mount was at 1900 hours, after which he was to pull a twelve-hour shift. When he reported to Whittle, the sergeant asked, "What are *you* doing here?"

"I'm reporting for duty, like you said. Don't you need me to sign in or something?"

"Did you go to personnel?"

"Yeah."

"Then we don't need you until seven. Bye."

When Liberty walked out the door, he considered whether it was worth his time to walk back to the barracks or if he should wait an hour for guard mount. While he was standing in a quandary, Tyler drove by on his way off-base. He pulled his gray and gold Jaguar to the side of the road and called, "Hey, Boatman! Want to go for a ride? I'm going to my apartment to change into my uniform."

Liberty ran the fifty feet to Tyler's car and got into the passenger's side. Tyler stepped on the gas and the two were off-base in a matter of seconds. Tyler said, "I live in Glyfada. That's where most of the Americans live. The American Bar is there and a beach full of cigarette butts, but a beach all the same. You'll like the hammers here. They got kind of sing-song voices that sound rather pleasant. If you learn Greek, you'll make out like a bandit. Have you tasted the meat here?"

"Yeah."

"How do you like it?"

"Tastes like swill."

"You'll come to love it. Just like the first time I saw the Greeks dipping their bread into olive oil. I thought it was pretty disgusting, but now I do it myself. After a while, you become more Greek than the Greeks."

They traveled at a good clip down a narrow road with huge trees lining either side of it. A bus pulled out directly in front of them. Liberty thought they were going a bit too fast as they came up with it when, quickly pumping his brakes, Tyler said, concerned but casually, "Hang on. I got no brakes."

Suddenly, the bus was the size of a barn. Tyler swerved right, saw a woman and two children on the sidewalk, and then made a crucial decision. He couldn't see around the bus but decided to risk a head-on collision. He pulled into the oncoming lane. Both men knew that it was death if there was a car there and both sucked in their breaths in anticipation. When the car cleared the bus, giving them a view down the road, they sighed with relief. They saw a couple of cars coming, but far enough away to allow them to successfully pass the bus. Tyler downshifted into first gear and coasted, using the hand brake when he had to come to a stop. He said, by way of explanation, "I didn't want to hit the people on the sidewalk."

Liberty said, "That's okay. I would've done the same thing."

Driving much more slowly, the two men finally reached Tyler's apartment. He said, looking carefully about, "Wait a minute." Then he said, "I guess it's okay."

Tyler led Liberty into his apartment. While he was in his bedroom changing, Liberty waited in the living room. There were no chairs. Instead, white flokati rugs, three inches thick and made from wool, covered the floor. Against one wall was a long coffee table with a stereo system sitting on it. In two corners of the room were large speakers and albums piled in disarray next to the nearby stereo. When Tyler was finished changing, the two men returned to base with five minutes to spare.

They joined the other cops and were issued their .38 Specials and eighteen rounds per man. Each cop was required to load his weapon at the clearing barrel. This was a red painted 55-gallon drum tilted up at a 45 degree angle which was filled with sand. In the center of the drum's cover was a small, empty, tin can. For safety, every weapon being either loaded or unloaded had its muzzle placed into the tin can.

As Liberty was loading his pistol, Whittle asked, "Boatman, how much training have you had?"

"I had on-the-job training at Minot, North Dakota."

"Did you go to tech school?"

"I already told you. No."

"So you've had no real training at all?"

"That's right."

"Can you shoot a gun?"

"Yep."

"Well, I'm the OJT trainer here and I'll give you all the training you need right now. If you have to shoot somebody, shoot to kill. Say that you shot for the legs, but make sure you kill your man. Otherwise, he'll press charges against you and you're the one who'll end up in jail. You might even consider carrying a knife as a plant: self defense."

"I'll remember that, Sarge."

Whittle then called, "Okay men, line up!"

Twelve men stood in a single, straight line in front of the police station. Except for Whittle and Sgt. Bubb, no one there was older than 24 years. Even though it was 80 degrees in the shade, most of them wore their short, olive green MA-1 jackets with their brilliant orange linings that reminded Liberty of native brook trout. The jackets were used like knapsacks. The many pockets carried the necessary items such as flashlights and notepads as well as forbidden items such as books and radios. Liberty had even sewed a huge pocket on the inside of his jacket to hold large textbooks.

Whittle looked down the line and asked, "Where's Wallich?"

A voice answered, "In the office."

Whittle called into the open door, "Wallich, get your ass out here!"

The man who had called Liberty a pig burst through the door and jumped into line. There was laughter in his eyes and a subtle smile on his lips when he saw Liberty.

Whittle ordered, "Attention!" The line straightened itself as Whittle walked its length. He said, "Wallich, shine your shoes. Finkbinder, wear a white tee shirt when in uniform. Siebold and Burrows, get haircuts. Tyler, never mind. You're just too ugly." Siebold broke rank as he fought his laughter. Whittle turned angrily, "Cut it out!" Siebold stiffened back into formation.

Whittle walked to the midpoint of the line, then faced it. He said, "Gents, in case you haven't noticed, we got a new man on the flight, Claudius Boatman. Show him the ropes. Finkbinder, you're desk sergeant. Wallich - main gate. Siebold and Beattie, pick up radios and your M-16s; you're on flight line patrol. Schlumberger, you and Burrows - Car Four. Tyler, you'll be humping the radio shack. The rest of you will be on foot patrol on the flight line. Pick up your M-16s. Boatman, you're with me. We're still working twelve hours on, twelve off, until the recall is over which may not be until next month. Any questions?" Whittle waited a moment before calling, "Post!"

The group broke up to go to their respective posts. Whittle said, "Boatman, we've got to escort payroll from the Ford Building in town. That's where the BX is located. It used to be a Ford factory." Whittle tossed him the keys to the flight chief's station wagon. "You drive."

Once they were both in the car, Whittle continued, "You'll notice that the tires squeal when you're making moderately fast turns. That's because the Greeks put marble into their asphalt." Whittle then slouched down and stretched out to enjoy the ride.

Liberty, who had been in the country less than three days, already felt the antipathy all GIs felt toward the gray Greek taxis. He refused to be intimidated by them or by anything else on the road. When an oncoming bus missed them by inches, Whittle sat up and said, "You like to play it close, don't you?"

When the highway was approaching downtown Athens, it changed from two lanes to one lane at an intersection with a light. At the red light, Liberty saw that the road suddenly narrowed and that a Greek taxi was edging out front to his left, he knew that he'd have to gun the engine to beat the taxi to the other side. When the light turned green, the taxi immediately pulled ahead and started to force Liberty to push to one side. It looked as though he would have to slow down and let the taxi win. However, Liberty was an inspired driver. He saw that no one was on the sidewalk. If he could manage to miss the pole, he might be able to cut the taxi off. Liberty hit the accelerator, pulled his car halfway onto the sidewalk, and when he judged that he was far enough ahead, he cut back onto the road and cut the taxi off while managing to miss the pole.

The taxi driver honked his horn furiously while Whittle yelled, "Are you crazy?"

Liberty said, "He cut me off, Sarge. I had to beat him. I had no choice."

"I don't care if he cut you off! I want to finish my tour here and go back to the world in one piece! If you want to kill yourself, do it on someone else's time, not mine! You got that?"

"Sure, Sarge I got it." Liberty watched the taxi in his rearview mirror, then asked, "Sarge, what does this mean?" He spread his fingers and motioned as though throwing an invisible ball.

"He's throwing you five. He's cursing you, your family, and all your ancestors and descendants."

"Okay, that's all right."

"Maybe for you, but not for them. Don't *you* go throwing curses around. They take it seriously."

They wove their way along the narrow streets of Athens. Whittle, as an afterthought, fastened his seat belt. Soon, they were on another highway. Liberty was in the passing lane when Whittle hurriedly said, pointing to a large yellow brick building, "There it is. We've almost passed it."

Liberty saw the monolith almost at a right angle to him and made a sharp right turn for its parking lot. Unknown to Liberty, a drainage ditch surrounded most of the parking lot. Since he missed the entrances and exits, the car crashed through the ditch. The car dived, then reared like a horse as it bounced halfway across the lot. Whittle's head smashed into the roof of the car, jamming his cap firmly onto his head. After he ripped his cap off, Whittle stared at Liberty, too bewildered to say a word. Liberty thought how Whittle's eyes looked like two huge, brilliant, blue gems in too small a setting.

Fighting for self-control, Whittle said in forced calm, "I want to tell you two things. First, I think you're really stupid. Second, I'm driving back to base before you kill us." Liberty stared impassively at Whittle and could see the alarm in his face.

At last, he spoke. "Okay, Sarge."

"That's it? 'Okay, Sarge.' That's it? You almost get us killed and that's it?"

"Well, yeah."

Whittle's jaw tightened. He threw open his car door and marched into the building. He returned accompanied by a Greek civilian carrying a small, brown, cloth bag. The Greek got into a compact car. Whittle opened the driver's door and said to Liberty, "Move over. *I'm* driving."

Liberty did as ordered. When the Greek started his car and pulled away, the police car followed. They were returning to the base with the day's profits. Liberty tried to excuse his driving and managed to begin several times by saying, "Sarge," but Whittle always cut him off. Finally, the sergeant said, "Boatman, don't say a word, not a freaking word!"

When they reached base, the Greek deposited the money into the police station safe. Liberty was happy when he was told to pull main gate with Peter Wallich. He found Whittle's brooding somewhat disconcerting.

To his relief, Wallich was reading, which meant he wouldn't have to make the effort to talk and be sociable. Pete hardly greeted Liberty when he entered the glass and aluminum shack. Liberty could sit, and think, and be alone with his thoughts. Pete would be temporarily nonexistent. After Liberty had waved a car through, Pete said to him, "You don't have to salute officers up here."

Liberty bent down to see what Pete was reading. He saw the title, *Thus Spake Zarathustra*. He thought, *another college dropout*, then said, "I hope you don't believe that superman crap. I used to believe in it, too, but then I realized that every Ivy League freak must think of himself as a superman. I once complained to a girlfriend that the federal government seemed to have nothing in it but Ivy League elitists. She said, 'Don't you want the best people running our government?' Uh huh. It's the best people in government who got us into the Vietnam War."

Wallich fidgeted in his seat and said, "I'm reading." For the most part, Liberty stood outside the shack and let him read. He put his hands in his pockets, crossed his legs, and leaned against the small building. An airman passed through the gate about fifteen feet away. He flashed his green ID card, to which Liberty nodded and let him pass. Whittle, who had been watching from the office, was instantly upon him. "Boatman! Did you check that man's ID card?"

Liberty straightened as he answered. "I sure did, Sarge."

"How could you see it from that far away?"

"I got the eyes of an eagle, Sarge."

Wallich chuckled. Whittle continued. "From now on, I want you to physically take the ID in your hands and actually read it. You can read, can't you?"

"I think so, Sarge."

"Get your hands out of your pockets!"

"Okay, Sarge."

"Wallich, do something with this idiot!"

"What?"

"Take him out and drown him!"

Liberty said, "I think that's against regs, Sarge."

Whittle turned and was on his way to the office when he glanced back and saw that Liberty had reinserted his hands into his pockets. He did an about face, marched up to him, and said, "Boatman, what did I just tell you?"

Liberty thought and thought and thought. Finally, he said, "I don't remember, Sarge."

"I told you to get your hands out of your pockets."

"Oh yeah, right." Liberty took his hands out of his pockets.

Whittle turned about, shaking his head in disbelief, and returned to the office. Liberty put his hands in his pockets, but quickly took them out again when he saw Whittle stop at the office door and threateningly put his hands on his hips, ready to march back to the gate.

Shortly before midnight, Liberty and Wallich were relieved from the gate. Whittle gave them a ride to the flight line, the real target of any serious assault. Wallich was teamed with Bob Siebold in a pickup truck and became the flight line roving patrol. Liberty was to guard one side of the flight line on foot.

Liberty and Whittle got out of the flight chief's station wagon. They walked to a metal helicopter pad. The sergeant said, "This is your post. You'll be here for the rest of the night."

Liberty looked around. The helicopter pad was surrounded by bare cement for a hundred feet each way. On the side nearest the

Greek airbase was a ditch filled with thick brush. He saw a small building a hundred yards away. He asked, "Sarge, what's that?"

"That's the boundary of the Greek airbase. There's a Greek guard in there. They have nothing to do with us." As Whittle started to walk to his car, Liberty called him back. "Hey, Sarge."

The sergeant returned. "What is it, Boatman?"

"I got no cover. I'm a sitting duck here."

"That's the idea. If you get killed, then we know we have infiltrators. Don't worry, Boatman, we'll get the bastards for you."

Liberty looked into Whittle's eyes. He could see that he was serious. He had thought lines like that were only good for the movies. Now they were being used on him. He wanted to ask, "Is that all my life is worth?" but he didn't think Whittle would understand. Besides, it was like being stunned by a well-placed punch. He was struck dumb by a sudden insight, the unimportance of his own life and, by extension, the unimportance of each individual life. He needed time to think. Whittle walked to his car and left the flight line.

As Liberty walked up and down the ramp, he knew he stood out as a dark, well-defined shadow against the lighter night sky and background light-all units. Ironically, it was peaceful and calm. The night and its stars couldn't be more beautiful. He remembered a story told about his great-grandfather Seitzer who had fought in the Civil War. He was only seventeen and was given picket duty where, nightly, every guard had been knifed to death. In the middle of the night, he heard a pig rooting in the woods. He was so frightened that he shot the pig. In the morning, it was discovered that the animal was a Confederate soldier.

Remembering this, Liberty approached the Greek guard shack as near as he safely could. Technically, he had left his post, but no one was there and he wanted to have some fun. He started imitating jungle sounds like the ones he had heard in Tarzan movies. After five minutes, he saw a small head peek around the corner of the Greek guard shack. Liberty said to himself, *pop, you're dead*. He returned to his post.

Wallich and Siebold occasionally checked on him to make sure he was awake and well and Tyler was good enough to bring him coffee from The Crossroads. However, Liberty was alone, totally alone, and that aloneness tasted like lead.

THE GROTTO

It was my day off. Normally, I would go to the gym and work out, and later go to the library to spend the rest of the day reading. I had a routine which I followed: read for two hours, take a twenty-minute coffee break, then read for another two hours.

Today, however, I wanted to go wild, to do something out of the ordinary. I could go to the Acropolis, which I still had not visited after living in Athens for over two years, but it was so close that I could see it another day, any day. Restlessly, I put on a light jacket to ward off the November chill and went to The Crossroads for lunch and to salivate over the dependent girls.

As I sat, eating, I was joined by Ken Tyler, a Creole from Louisiana. His strong, handsome face burst in a shower of smiles as he turned a chair around and sat facing its back. He rested his chin on his muscular arms, which in turn were sitting on the top of the backrest. Like me, he wore sneakers and blue jeans, but I wore a regular shirt beneath my jacket while he wore a white, sleeveless tee-shirt like the kind worn by grandfathers and weightlifters.

He greeted me. "What's happening?"

I answered, "Nothing, but I want to do something. Anything. But I don't know what."

He said, "I just got done pumping up my arms." He flexed his biceps. "Look good, don't they?"

I felt my own arms diminish in size as I agreed with him.

Ken made a smacking sound with his lips while he seemed lost in thought. He said, "I got the day off, too. Want to go mountain climbing?"

"Where?"

"Voula Mountain. We can—" He interrupted himself. He lifted an arm the thickness of a telephone pole, waved, and called, "Hi, Tina!"

I turned and saw a small, petite, blond girl with unusually large breasts that perked proudly though the thin fabric of her blouse. I swallowed my lust, took a deep breath, and faced Ken.

He continued. "We can check out the cliffs facing the base. I hear there are lots of caves up there."

I said, "There are. I've been there, but you just gave me an idea. I know where there's an underwater cave, a grotto. I still have to explore it. It's near Sounion. Want to go?"

I watched another dependent girl, with the same high yellow skin color and intelligent brown eyes as Ken, sneak up behind him. Stealthily, she wrapped an arm about his neck. He pretended surprise, then laughed, took her hand, and kissed it. She brought her hand down and rubbed his chest. She asked, "Can I touch these?"

He answered, "Only if I can touch yours."

She kissed him lightly on his ear and left for the Annex, a magazine/bookstore abutting The Crossroads.

I asked sharply, "What is it with you, anyway!"

He laughed. It was then that Craig Crofoot wandered into the cafeteria. He seemed a little disjointed and probably just got out of bed. As he sat down, I said, "Ken and I are going to explore an underwater cave. Want to come along?"

"Naw, I've got to work tonight. An underwater cave, huh?"

"Yeah, it's going to be great fun!"

He said, still a little groggy, "Be careful of those squiggly things."

I was immediately suspicious. "What squiggly things?"

"The things that grab your legs when you're swimming and pull you under. Last week there was a story in the paper about a diver who got caught by something and was held under water until his scuba tank ran out of air. About once a month there's some kind of story about someone being pulled down to his death."

"You know," I said skeptically, "I read the papers all the time and not once, not once, do I remember ever reading a story about a diver getting pulled down to his death like that."

"It's not only divers. People out for a swim get it, too. Some of those octopuses get awful big."

"If you're trying to scare me, it's not going to work."

"What about those old pictures of sailing ships being attacked by giant squids? That's real. That came from somewhere. Modern ships are too fast and big to be grabbed like that, but a swimmer is fresh meat."

"Craig, you've got a good imagination. It's amazing what your pretend world can dream up."

"Okay, I tried to warn you. Don't blame me if you're pulled down like a drowning rat!"

"We're leaving, Crofoot, and it's not going to work."

"What?"

"Let's go, Ken."

We decided to use my beat-up, blue Volkswagen bug, which I had named Old Blue. I thought this odd since he had a nicer car, a '64 silver-and-gold Jaguar. I thought, at first, that he might be afraid of it since he nearly rear-ended a bus when the car's brakes gave.

First, we went to my place off-base where I changed into a bathing suit, just in case the water was warm enough for a swim. I slipped my blue jeans on over the swimsuit and picked up a towel. We then drove to Tyler's place.

As soon as we parked by the curb, I knew something was wrong. Quicker than a cough, Ken ducked below the dashboard to hide his face. He hissed, "There she is!"

I looked across the road toward his apartment complex and saw a tall, thin Greek woman about forty years of age. She walked across the lawn and into the door of an adjacent building. I was confused and asked, "What's wrong?"

Ken asked, "Is she gone?"

I answered, after looking carefully about us, "I don't see anyone. If you're talking about the Greek woman, she's gone, too."

He sat up. I looked at the hard-muscled man next to me and asked, "What's this all about?" I didn't know what to think.

He was hesitant. He was forcing himself to speak. "Because … because …" He stopped, then made his decision. "She's my landlady. I pay my rent by pooning her."

I was stunned. I knew Ken was good, but here was a man of movie-star caliber, of Hollywood dimensions! He might have been a Black super-athlete or a member of a British rock group! Envious joy and awe filled my heart. My body thrilled and my groin tightened. I said, "Aw, man! What a deal! She's not bad looking either!"

Tyler sighed. "Yeah, it sounds sweet, but it's not. At first it was great, but now she's screwing me to death. I never get any rest. I have no personal life. I never have time for any real dates with the women my own age. Every time I'm home, she comes in and we screw. I work all day and screw all night. I never get any sleep. I don't even know what she'd do if I brought a hammer home."

This time it was my turn to laugh. I mocked, "Gee, sounds tough to me."

"You don't understand. I can't let her see me. We'll have to sneak into my apartment."

We got out of Old Blue and crouched behind her. Commando-like, Tyler whispered, "When I say go, run for the door on the right. Hang back a couple of seconds so I'll have time to unlock the door."

Tyler watched the adjacent building for signs of life. Its windows and doors stared blankly at us. He yelled, "Go!"

I watched him lumber with his weightlifter legs toward his door, one house running toward another house. I counted, "One thousand one, one thousand two," then I sprang forward to make my bid for safety.

I don't remember everything that happened. I remember the sweat running down my face. I remember breathing heavily with every step I took. I remember the harsh glare of the sun half-blinding me. I gritted my teeth and murmured, "I can make it. I can make it."

Ken and I reached the door at the same time. While he fumbled with his keys, I danced up and down like a cartoon cat running over broken glass. He finally inserted his key, threw the door open, and the two of us threw ourselves onto the flokati rugs layering the floor. We could not have been more determined had bullets been whining by our heads or grenades popping to the right and left of us.

Ken retrieved his swimsuit and towel and threw them into a clear plastic bag. He said, "I'll change later." He then put on a jacket after admitting that he, too, was cold.

I said with mock seriousness, "Let's rock and roll."

In a moment, we were rushing toward Old Blue. We kept our heads down as though his landlady could not see us. In another moment, we were racing away toward Sounion and high adventure.

After half an hour of driving along the top of a seaside cliff-hugging road, we came to a blunted finger of land pointing toward Salamis and Persian defeat. It was here that I stopped the car. Directly across a small bay and facing us was Sounion, where Theseus' father plunged into eternity. To our right was a small pimple of rock too far out to swim to.

I led the way to the water. We had to climb over a desert-like terrain sporting small, scrubby-looking bushes and sparse grass trying to make a living on denuded, bare rock. We climbed down the craggy rocks, some of which crumbled at our touch, until we were at the water's edge. Both of us dipped our fingers into the water. I said, "It's far too cold and rough for a swim."

Ken flexed his pectoral muscles. He said, "Maybe for some."

I knew he was joking so I ignored him. We followed a path that centuries of beachcombing had made. To our left was a small cliff, about ten feet high, consisting of tumbled boulders. To our right, about two feet away, was the Aegean Sea, with a depth, at this point, of at least fifteen feet.

We continued along the path until it widened to a small, cliff-enclosed beach that had a cave at the far end. Here, a good part of the rock had been washed away so that only the harder, more de-fiant rock remained. Odd, natural sculptures stood thirty feet high and made a wonderland maze through which the path wound.

Once past the cave, the path again followed the foot of the seaside cliffs except that the cliffs were getting progressively steeper and taller. The haphazard boulders had given way to a sandstone face a hundred feet high. We followed the path until we could go no further. I paused and said, "Listen."

We heard a deep, distant rumbling. Tyler said, "It sounds like a thunderstorm except that there aren't any clouds."

"That's the grotto." I pointed to the cliff face a couple of feet beyond the path's end. A black triangle, three feet high, jutted above the water line. I said, "That's the top of the grotto. The rest of it is underwater. If you get close enough, the thunder you hear sounds like people talking in an echo chamber."

We bent over the cave mouth as much as we could from our rocky perch. I asked, "What do you think? I had hoped one of us could go in, but the water's too cold and I forgot a flashlight."

We could see vague shadows and outlines from light reflect-ed off the water. Although I didn't mention Crofoot's warning, I asked, "Do you think anything lives in there, you know, something that might grab your legs?"

With confidence, Ken said, "I know there are sharks around, but I doubt if they hang out here. Octopuses won't attack you. I think you're safe."

His attitude of total control annoyed me, so I said, "Good! Let's see you dangle your legs in the water!"

He retorted, "Let's see you dangle *your* legs in the water! This is your cave, not mine."

"That means that if I find a treasure, it's all mine, right?"

For emphasis, Ken hit his chest with a mighty fist and said, "Hey, I'm here, ain't I?"

At this point the sandstone cliff was a hundred feet high. I studied the area, hoping I could find some way to cancel the combined effects of the shadows and reflections. I noticed that the sandstone cliff extended fifteen feet beyond the cave mouth. Here it abruptly gave way to a limestone cliff just as high and steep, but with a much smoother surface.

Also, at this point of transition was a small, flat rock that formed a natural dock about ten feet long and three feet wide. It jutted into the water perpendicular to the cliff face. I thought that if I could reach this rock by climbing over the cave, I could look into the cave at a different angle. I thought I might even find some Persian treasure.

I explained my plan to Ken and, bemused, he silently watched me mount the cliff face. At first, the climb was easy. Small pieces of rock stuck out from the sandstone and I used these as grips to spider my way toward the cave mouth. I hugged the cliff, stomach pressing forcefully against the stone, hands and feet fumbling for supports. I inched my way up and across until I was directly over the cave mouth and ten feet from the boiling water.

Ken warned, "Be careful, Guy. Those grips look none too strong."

I carefully turned my head toward him, pressing it against the sandstone. I gritted my teeth and said, moving only my lips, "I have four grips. What are the chances of any two breaking at the same time?"

That stopped him cold, until three of my grips snapped off simultaneously. Down, down I plummeted, my body scraping the cliff like provolone down a cheese grater. The turmoil of the water and the turmoil in my mind were a perfectly matching pair as I found myself ten feet below the surface and still not touching bottom.

Fortunately, I am a good swimmer. With a couple of strong strokes, I exploded up to my waist out of the water and gasped for air. When gravity pulled me back to my neck, I swam with forceful strokes to my original destination, the flat rock. I pulled myself onto it.

Alarmed, Ken called, "Are you okay?"

I stood up and answered, "Yeah, I'm all right."

As his concern gave way to relief, Ken laughed. "Hee, hee, hee. You look like a stranded rat I once saw during a flood. How ya gonna get back?"

"I don't know. I want to check out the cave first." I tried to see inside from this new angle, but to no effect. Pretending to be intent on the cave, I surreptitiously edged a finger to the bridge of my nose. When I pulled my finger away, there was blood at the tip of it. My fingers had small scratches on them, and my stomach and chest burned. I decided to check them out once I was away from Ken and back in my apartment.

I said, "I can't see anything from here." Hoping that this sounded casual enough, I pretended to unconsciously scratch myself while in reality feeling for wounds. I could have admitted, "Ken, I'm hurt," but that would have been too simple. Here was big, strong, happy Ken watching my every move. How could I have admitted weakness in front of him?

Ken reiterated, "How ya gonna get back?"

I snapped, "I guess I'll fly!" I caught myself and added, "I suppose I could dive to you." We both looked at the large, subsurface rocks separating us. I couldn't judge their depths and certainly didn't want to dive headfirst into one of them. I said, "Let's forget *that* idea."

One glance at the cliff told us that I could never get out that way. I didn't want to chance another swim.

After some thought, I said excitedly, "I've got it! I'll jump into the water for buoyancy. That'll partially support my weight. Then I can crawl back to you along the sandstone cliff with half my body in the water and half of it out. The grips won't break because they'll support only half my weight while the water supports the other half. What'd you think?"

Ken shrugged and his head almost disappeared in the mass of his shoulder muscles. He said, "Go for it."

I thought of stripping, but I didn't think I could reach Ken by throwing my wet clothes the fifty feet between us. Since I was already soaked, I jumped into the water fully clothed.

I began my voyage along the foot of the cliff and thought my idea was going to work. Then the first wave hit. It smashed me bodily against the cliff. When I bounced off, an undertow, which I had not noticed before, grabbed me and pulled me under, trying to rip me from the land. All my concentration went into my fingers as they closed viselike on their holds. My whole body was submerged except for those courageous fingers that refused to release their tenuous grips.

In the pause between the outgoing and incoming waves I catapulted to the surface, gulped some air, and moved three inches toward Tyler when another wave overwhelmed me. Again, I was smashed against the cliff then sucked underwater. Again, I lunged for air and inched toward my partner.

I was yoyo-ed like this until I was directly in front of the cave mouth. My arms were stretched way above my head to compensate for the three feet of free space where the cave reached above the water line. I felt as though my wrists were tied and I was being tormented in a weird bondage ritual.

I had been systematically averting my face, but it had taken quite a beating and was bleeding from a number of small, bruised cuts. Although my injuries thus far were minor, they felt horrible and I envisioned my face as looking like ground hamburger.

I was scared. I was already exhausted and was fighting panic caused by my struggles for air. As my legs dangled before the cave, a new fear set in. With fresh insight, I suddenly knew what was in the cave: a hideous beast, all arms, legs, and teeth and covered by green, decaying algae; a beast hungry for meat, man meat.

I caught my breath and tried to calm myself. Then I thought what a tempting feast I must present with my legs tantalizingly waving before cold, dully calculating, fisheyes. I could see my legs being pulled like bell cords as I was dragged to the depths below. Only a bubbled, smothered gurgle would erupt from my mouth before I would lie, dead, in the suckered arms of The Beast.

I would have screamed in earnest when I heard, "Hee, hee hee! That's the way, babe!"

Oddly, Ken's laughter snapped me out of my panic. Kicking wildly, hoping I'd knock out The Beast before it got to me, and straining my every muscle, I fought my way past the cave. A handful of dunkings brought me close enough for Ken to reach down and pull me out of the water.

Surprised and concerned, he said, "I'm sorry. I didn't know you were in trouble. I thought you were busting me. Are you all right?"

I tottered on my feet and said, "Barely."

Ken said, "Your face looks something awful. Are you sure you're okay?"

When I nodded yes, he hugged me in his earth moving arms. He happily exploded, "I'm glad you made it, buddy. You should have seen yourself. You were great! Hee, hee, hee."

I borrowed Ken's clear plastic bag that contained his swim trunks and towel. I stripped off all of my wet clothes except my trousers and sneakers and put them into the bag.

We started for the car. As we retraced our steps, we met two Greek couples. They were lying on the sand of the small beach amongst the stylus-like rocks pointing toward the sky. Both couples seemed to be in love. Happiness sparkled in their eyes.

While we were passing them, one of the young men asked, in Greek, "Were you fishing?" They burst into laughter. I knew they had seen me.

I answered in Greek, "No, I not fish."

They laughed some more.

I turned toward Ken and, exasperated, whined in English, "I don't need this."

Instead of the expected sympathy, I heard, "Hee, hee, hee."

SCHLUMBERGER

One oven-hot, baking afternoon, I was headed onto Athenai Air-base to attend a mandatory race relations class. Although the class got me out of regular duty, it was onerous and, like almost all the white GIs, I regarded it with bitter resentment. To most of us, it was harassment designed to humiliate whites in an effort to force them to accept, not the equality of Blacks, but the transformation of white guys into second-class citizens.

That afternoon, Frank Schlumberger was pulling the main gate. In addition to his clean blue uniform and shiny white cap, he wore a pair of dark, regulation sunglasses that made his head look like that of an oversized ant.

Frank was an enigma. Of all the thousands of people I have met in my life, he is the only one who was universally disliked. Both lifers and non-lifers, normally hostile groups, hated him. I would look at his childish face, his quiet blue eyes, short black hair, and light skin and think, *he's just like me*. I couldn't help but wonder why he was so hated.

As I was walking through the gate, he called to me, "Hey, Guy! I noticed you're getting four days off."

31

I asked, "What are you talking about?"

"You're going back to night shift next week, right? I noticed that between your last race relations class and your first night shift, they've given you four days off."

I smiled. "That's great! Good for me!"

"Yeah, but unless you're on leave, taking four days off is against the regs. You're only allowed three days off."

Suspicious, I asked, "What's that to you?"

"I think you should report it, don't you? If you don't report it, I will. Regs are regs. They weren't written for the fun of it."

I didn't know what to do. I hoped he was joking, but later that day, he walked into the back office and I was ordered to report for work a day early.

A month after this, we had one of our bimonthly recalls. Arab terrorists had threatened the base, but they did it so often that it had almost become a routine, hardly worth a passing comment. Police flights were doubled and everyone pulled twelve-hour shifts. Tech Sergeant Tom Whittle's flight was combined with Staff Sergeant Anthony Frick's flight for the night shift.

That night, while waiting for guard mount, I was sitting in the outer office of the police station. A handful of us were there and we were all furious at the terrorists for the extra hours we'd have to work. It was even more aggravating to know that the death of any of us would be a meaningless statement and would change, literally, nothing.

Bob Siebold lumbered into the room from the outside. He put his coffee on the desk and said, "I feel like a dung beetle." He paused for the comment to sink in and waited for someone to ask him why he felt like a dung beetle. When no one offered the expected question, he continued, "Someone keeps throwing sand onto my ball of crap and I'm always cleaning it off." Finkbinder, with bemused wonder, mouthed the word, "What?" behind his back as Siebold's laughter rumbled through the room.

Bob then walked restlessly to the outside door. While he stood there, looking into the dark, with a hand on either side of the doorjamb, Schlumberger quickly replaced Bob's Styrofoam cup with one of his own. Before any of us could react, Bob reached down for his coffee and brought it to his lips. In that instant his whole body convulsed. I could see the muscles on his face tighten as he made a tremendous effort at self-control. Despite this, he dropped the cup and a toad hopped out of it.

Schlumberger was the first to laugh and the rest of us joined him. Bob's sky-blue eyes scanned the group and landed on Schlumberger. The strain of self-control was evident. The lines of Bob's face stretched and hardened, but he didn't say a word. Schlumberger said, "Surprised you, didn't I? I thought it'd be pretty funny. You should have seen your face!"

Bob said in a controlled whisper, "I want my coffee."

I could see the startled excitement in Bob's eyes and I thought, *in another time and in another place, Frank would be dead.* When Frank gave him his coffee, Bob left the office and I sighed deeply with relief. Schlumberger simply didn't know the chance he had taken.

A few minutes later, Sergeant Whittle called guard mount. Most of the posts were doubly manned with extra people. Instead of working main gate alone, I was teamed up with Bob Siebold. It would be a good night for me. Claudius Boatman, unfortunately, was paired with Frank Schlumberger on base patrol.

No one liked to be a passenger in any vehicle driven by Claudius, so it wasn't unusual when Frank jumped into the driver's seat of an Air Force pickup truck without even a second glance at Liberty. Normally, when he was alone on base patrol, Liberty would find a dark, quiet corner where he could read and perhaps take a nap. With Frank in the car, he would have to at least make a pretense of working. They first checked the guards to make sure they had enough coffee to keep them awake until post change. Next, they checked the doors of designated buildings to make sure they were all properly locked for the night, a procedure Liberty followed only when he wanted to break into a place himself. From experience, he knew that over the course of a year, every building would eventually have an unlocked door or an open window.

They were doing their rounds when Frank said, "I'm as tough as you are." Liberty looked at the small, thin figure and studied the boyish face. Frank reiterated, "I'm as tough as you are."

Liberty shrugged. "Sure, if you say so."

As they checked the commander's office and the BX, Frank said, "When I was growing up, we were pretty tough kids. We'd put bread out for the birds, then shoot them from the cellar windows when they came for the bread. The pellet guns were okay, but the .22s made your ears ring when you fired them in the house."

Liberty listened silently.

Frank continued, "Sometimes we'd catch a gopher. We'd tie a rope around its neck, break its legs, then throw it into the water." Frank chuckled, not maliciously, but joyously. "You should have seen it. It was so funny to watch it toss and turn while it was trying to swim. You see, we'd keep it from drowning by keeping its head above the water with the rope."

Frank waited for Liberty to react, but he was met with only brooding silence. Oblivious of the impression he was making, he said, "I wasn't the best shot, but no one fooled with me. I once saw an interview with a man who used to target shoot with Billy the Kid. He said that he could outshoot Billy any day, but that he wouldn't have a chance against him in a real gunfight. I'm like that. I might be small, but toughness isn't measured by size. No one messes with me."

They pulled into the parking lot of the legal office. The building was being renovated. The unpainted front door was half open. Some of the windows were newly installed and still wore stickers advertising their makers. Other windows leaned lazily against the side wall of the building, awaiting their turns at installation. Nails, cinder blocks, and metal bars lay haphazardly about, all covered by a fine, white layer of dust.

Despite this, work at the office had never stopped. The rooms were still occupied by large desks covered by reams of paper which had yet to be sifted, deciphered, and filed. Chairs, typewriters, and other office paraphernalia littered the room.

Both men were surprised to see a police sedan sitting before the small, square, gray building. Its lights were on and Liberty could see Anthony Frick, one of the two flight chiefs on duty, rummaging through the desk drawers. He could see a second person, maybe Tom Whittle, the other flight chief, also rummaging though the office.

Frank asked, "What are they doing?"

Before Liberty could answer, Frick looked out the office window and glowered at them. His lips moved and the other man stopped all activity. Frick was a big man and was the Black counterpart of Tom Whittle except that Frick, like Liberty, seemed to have a primal fierceness about him. His smile was really a sneer. A casual nod of recognition was more like a nod to an executioner to go ahead and kill. He marched to Frank's side of the truck although Liberty was the closer of the two. His smoldering eyes scanned the two men. Liberty's hard, gray eyes clashed with Frick's black, depthless eyes, metal on metal, hate against hate.

Frick shoved his brutal face into Frank's window and Liberty stifled his own lunge at the imperative head whose very existence seemed to insult him. Frick gnashed his jaws, then hissed, "Schlumberger, why didn't you check this door? I've been waiting here for half the night to see if you're doing your job. You should be checking this building every half hour. Sergeant Whittle told you about this place at guard mount, yet it took you all this time to get here! That's a dereliction of duty!"

Tears welled in Frank's eyes. His lower lip quivered, and he flushed red.

Liberty, on the other hand, was deadly quiet, a pit bull about to attack. Frank's inane stories had already violated his sense of right and wrong and now Frick, another man he disliked, was about to push. He could feel himself coming alive with excitement. His

breathing was shallow, and his groin thrilled with the coming con-
flict. If Frick said one word to him, Liberty would arrest him. If Frick
resisted at all, he would be shot, and Liberty's mind quickly ran
through scenarios where he could force Frick to go for his gun.

The flight chief paused in his tirade and looked carefully at
Claudius who, in turn, stared directly back. One killer instinctively
knows another killer. Liberty kept thinking, praying, *C'mon, c'mon,
go for me!* But Frick knew his danger. One look at Liberty told him
all he needed to know. It told him to back down.

Turning toward Frank, the flight chief hissed, "Schlumberger, if anything is stolen, it'll be your fault!"

When Frick returned to the office, the tension was broken,
and Liberty sighed with relief because the moment had passed. He
asked, "Why'd you let him talk to you that way?"

"What way?"

"What do you mean 'what way?' Like you were a piece of
crap."

Frank explained, "He was right. I was wrong. We should've
checked the building right away. It takes a brave man to admit when
he's wrong."

They finished their rounds by checking the laundromat, the
customs office, and the bowling alley. All were locked and safe for
the night. When it was post change, Schlumberger drove to the main
gate where they were to relieve Bob Siebold and me. Frank parked
next to the metal-framed, Plexiglas booth and said, "I'm gonna get
my briefcase at the office. I left it there before guard mount."

Liberty joined us and the three of us watched Schlumberger
walking to the office. Bob said, "Look how he puckers up his butt
like a bantam rooster." He started his rumbling laughter, but suddenly reached up to massage his temples. He said, "Ah, my head! It
feels like the Great Rift Valley. Ever since that twerp pulled his joke
with the toad, I've had a splitting headache."

Liberty asked, "Did you guys notice anything unusual?"

Bob and I thought a moment, then I volunteered, "Yeah, we saw Frick and Whittle loading cardboard boxes into their cars."

The lines of Liberty's mouth lengthened as he told us what he and Frank had seen at the legal office.

I summarized. "They were ripping off the legal office!"

"Yeah."

Nothing more needed to be said. The three of us were safe. Frick nor Whittle would ever be able to court-martial us for any offense without running the risk of being charged with theft.

Schlumberger started his strut from the office to the gate. Liberty pointed to a low, flat-roofed building directly across the highway from the gate. He said, "That's a perfect place for a sniper."

I said, "I'm not going to worry about it, especially since you'll be here instead of me."

Liberty said, "Let's hope he shoots Schlumberger first."

When morning arrived, the recall was called off and the flights were disbanded. Each man went either to the barracks or to his off-base apartment to sleep until the afternoon when his normal routine commenced.

That evening at seven o'clock I was in Peter Wallich's room. I sat on the extra bunk, on which he stored his books in two long rows. I was surrounded by hundreds of books which he had bought at the American Bookstore in Athens. My weight sank the middle of the mattress so that the books all leaned toward me in disarray. I imagined Bob Siebold as saying, in a similar situation, "I felt like a pupa in a tight cocoon."

I like to read series of books, especially popular encyclopedias on specialized topics. They offer so much detail that, when I'm through, I feel like an expert in that field. If I read a fictional series, then I feel as though I've actually lived with the characters in the stories. I had already worked my way through the Time/Life books on nature and now I was reading the Mandingo series.

Liberty was in the room, too. He half-sat, half-lay in the one lounge chair in the room. One long leg was draped over an arm of the chair. The other leg was stretched straight out in front of him. He was reading a translation of Husserl's *Ideas*. He'd read a paragraph, look up with unseeing eyes that seemed to be looking through the opposite wall, then he'd read another paragraph.

Pete was hunched over his desk reading *Time* magazine. It was as though he was in a library. He was very attentive and seemed to believe that he could find truth, the truth, in the words of journalists. When he was done with *Time*, I knew he would turn to *Newsweek* and start perusing that with the same avidity.

Pete said to the room at large, "McGovern says that if he's elected, he's going to fall on his knees and beg the North Vietnamese for forgiveness."

Without looking up from Husserl, Liberty grabbed his groin with his right hand, shook it, and said, "That's what I think of McGovern. You'd have to put a gun to my head before I'd vote for that sucker."

Pete's lower jaw dropped. Visibly upset, he asked, "How can you say that? We're in the middle of an unjust war, and he wants to pull us out of it. That makes good sense to me."

Liberty looked up and made eye contact with Pete. He said, "First of all, the guy's a moron. Secondly, if we pull out now, we'll be betraying all the soldiers who have already died there, not to mention our Vietnamese allies."

"It's worth pulling out if you can save one life."

"Don't you mean one American life? The fact is, Pete, you're going to die, I'm going to die, every living thing on earth except bacteria is going to die. It's not the dying that's horrible, it's the dying for nothing. If we pull out now, all those people will have died for nothing."

I was amazed at how calm Liberty was. Usually, he'd be screaming and nearly frothing at the mouth if he was opposed, but he liked and respected Pete.

Just then, Dennis Finkbinder burst into the room. He said, "Schlumberger has taken an overdose! He seemed depressed and I saw him taking these pills!" Dennis held up two empty pill boxes. "I can't find him anywhere!"

Pete asked, "Did you call the office?"

"Yes, I did. They're looking for him now."

Pete suggested, "Why don't you go the dispensary to see what he took?"

"Good idea." Finkbinder ran down the hall.

Pete asked, "Should we look for him?"

Liberty answered, "I'm not wasting *my* time on that twerp. Take my word for it: the whole thing is bogus. You'll see."

"Does that mean, Mr. Compassion, that you're not going to help us?"

"That's exactly what it means."

Pete asked me if I wanted to look for Frank. I really didn't want to, yet I thought it was the right thing to do, especially since I didn't want to look bad in Pete's eyes.

Using Pete's Volkswagen, we drove to the dispensary where we met Finkbinder and Ken Tyler, who was on duty. Pete asked, "Any news?"

Tyler answered, "The gate guard saw Frank leaving base about ten minutes ago. He was walking."

Finkbinder added, "The medic said that these pills won't hurt him, even in massive doses, but that we should get him in here just in case. He may have taken other pills."

Even though we knew a patrol vehicle was looking for Frank, Pete and I decided to head into town and look for him ourselves. We drove out the gate and took a left toward Athens. We had followed the brilliant streetlights for two miles when we saw Frank sitting disconsolately on the sidewalk with his back against a stone wall. As soon as he spotted us, he stood up and hopped onto the wall. He walked along its top, balancing himself with his arms spread out like a tightrope performer. When we stopped near him, he seemed surprised.

Pete jumped out of his car and rushed toward him. I opened my door and stood next to it, half-expecting to chase Frank down. Pete ordered in a stern voice, "Get into the car!"

Instead of running, Schlumberger said coyly, like a little girl, "Okay."

We raced directly to the dispensary. We marched him in, one of us on either side of him. When the medic at the desk saw him, he said, "Oh, it's you."

Before further comment was made, an extremely handsome, youthful doctor escorted Frank into an examining room. Pete faced the medic and asked, "Do you know him?"

"Yeah. He came in here a few hours ago and asked me what would happen if he accidentally took an overdose of some pills he had. Like a dummy, I told him that I didn't think anything would happen. I didn't know he'd pull a stunt like this."

The doctor came out of the examination room. He said, "I don't think there's anything to worry about, but there's no need to take chances. We're going to keep him here overnight under observation."

Pete said, "Thank you, sir."

When we returned to Pete's room, Liberty was still there, comfortably reading. As we entered, he asked, "Well?"

Pete said, "I think we saved his life."

Liberty looked carefully at us. He could see our chagrin. He said, "Liar," and resumed his reading.

THE CHASE

Shortly before the night shift guard mount, Guy pulled his dusty, dented Volkswagen bug, Old Blue, into the row of similarly dented, dusty and earthy vehicles. From his car, he could see that Ken Tyler and Frank Schlumberger were arguing. Members of the oncoming flight loitered in the dark shadows of the night and watched the altercation. Guy heard Ken, who was about to be relieved, yell threateningly, "Don't you ever rat on me again!"

Guy wondered at Ken's anger since he was so casual about everything. Self-righteously, Frank asserted himself. "Uh, when you leave a dirty vehicle for your relief, uh, you're going against security police policy, uh, not to mention Air Force regulations."

"Are you relieving me?"

"Uh, no."

"So what business is it of yours?"

Frank calmly explained, "It's everybody's business. Uh, it's security police policy. I'm trying to enforce, uh, security police policy. Your vehicle, uh, upon your relief from duty, should be as clean, uh, as when you received it."

Tyler was enraged. "You turned me in because of a candy wrapper?"

"Filth is filth."

"But a candy wrapper? It wasn't even *my* candy wrapper! It was there when I relieved Pettenkoffer."

"Then you should have called *him* in and we wouldn't be having this conversation. Uh, it became your responsibility, uh, when you accepted the car from him."

Tyler stomped to his car and stopped briefly at Old Blue. He said, "I hate that rat! He's the only man – man? He's the only," and here he snarled, "*boy* I've ever met that both lifers and non-lifers absolutely hate. The back office hates him as much as *we* do."

As Guy got out of Old Blue, he said, "I don't hate him. It's like hating a maggot because he's a maggot. It's his nature to be a scum bucket and nothing's going to change that. By the way, what's with this 'uh' crap?"

Pete Wallich stepped from the shadows. "Schlumberger found out that Lawrence Welk was from his, uh, hometown."

Guy said, "Poor Frank. You see? He has no sense of identity. He's a maggot and nothing more. He's simply not worth hating."

That night the flight was introduced to a jeep, military slang for a new guy, named Richard Victor, a half Cherokee airman from Alabama, the third Cherokee in the security police. It seemed to Guy, who was always running into American Indians, particularly from the southern states, that half the Indian nation was in the U.S. military.

This was Rich's first duty assignment. That night he pulled flight line with Guy. Bob Siebold pulled main gate, Pete Wallich pulled base patrol, Schlumberger was the desk sergeant, and Whittle was the flight chief.

Guy drove to the flight line where he and Rich relieved the two cops already there. Once they exchanged their car for the pickup truck, Guy keyed the mike and said, "Car Three to Control, radio check."

Schlumberger called back, "I, uh, read you loud and clear. How do you, uh, read me?"

"Loud and clear." Guy replaced the mike back onto its receiver. Usually, the first radio check of the night was the last radio check unless the desk sergeant went "by the book" where he'd call the posts every hour.

Guy turned on the dome light and said to Rich, "We're not supposed to read on guard duty, but I do. We're also not supposed to listen to radios or sleep, but they have to catch us first. I'm going to read. If you want to rack out, go ahead. I'll watch."

Despite the fact that Rich was new to the Air Force, he immediately fit in as though he'd seen twenty years of service. He took off his shoes, unbuttoned his shirt, undid his belt, and half-reclined in his seat with his legs wide open, like a frustrated whore. In two minutes, his head bounced onto the back of his seat. His mouth dropped open and he started to snore. He looked so unkempt, even by Guy's standards, that he felt a rush of disgust. He fought the impulse to slap Rich awake and tell him to get decent.

An hour later, at midnight, Guy heard over the radio, "Uh, Control to Car Three."

Guy keyed the mike as Rich briefly stirred out of his trance. "Three by."

"Radio check."

"I read you loud and clear. How do you read me?"

"Uh, loud and clear."

At one o'clock Guy's reading was again interrupted. "Uh, Control to Car Three."

He keyed the mike. "Three by."

"Radio check."

"I read you loud and clear."

"I read you loud and clear, too." Then Schlumberger caught himself and added after a brief pause, "Uh."

Guy returned the mike to its receiver and said to himself, "Yeah, right, uh."

It was almost two o'clock in the morning when Guy heard a high buzzing sound rip out of the night to his left, the direction of the civilian airport. He flashed on the truck's headlights to see a nondescript dark man on a motorcycle dash through his light beams and into the night on his right. He hit Rich on the chest and said, "Wake up. We got an intruder." He jammed the pickup into gear and started the chase. As Rich tied his shoelaces and buttoned his shirt, Guy called on the radio, "Car Three to Control, be advised that we have an intruder on the flight line, either a Greek national or an Arab. Get Car Two and Car Four down here ASAP!"

Schlumberger said, "Ten twenty? I can't read you, uh."

"Be advised we have an intruder on the flight line. Get Car Two and Car Four down here. I'm going to cut him off at Base Ops!"

"Ten twenty? I can't read you."

"What do you mean you can't read me? You've been reading me loud and clear all night!"

"Ten twenty?"

A hard edge entered Guy's voice. Barely in control, he said, "I've got an intruder. Get Car Two and Car Four down here."

"I can't read you. You'll have to ten twelve from Base Ops."

"I'm in the middle of a chase! I can't call you from Base Ops! Get Car Two and Car Four down here!"

"Ten twenty? You'll have to ten twelve from Base Ops."

Guy threw the mike into the dashboard and swore, "Incompetent asshole!" In another moment, he trapped the intruder in a corner of the flight line just before he reached Main Base Road. The short, dark civilian stopped with the motorcycle resting between his legs.

Both cops hopped out of the pickup as soon as it stopped. Guy stood behind the truck for cover and expected Rich to do the same. Instead, the jeep ran up to the stranger with his hands cupped into a square, asking repeatedly, "Passo? Passo?"

Guy winced and waited to see if Rich was going to be dropped. He was so close to the stranger that he could have been killed with a knife. When Guy saw that Rich was still alive despite such a great opportunity for death, he left his cover. Rich brought him the stranger's I.D. Guy recognized it as a Greek policeman's identification card. He returned to the truck and called, "Car Three to Control."

Schlumberger answered, "Control by."

"We've apprehended what appears to be a Greek national on the flight line. Get Car Two down here."

"Ten twenty? You'll have to ten twelve from Base Ops."

Cursing, he threw down the mike. In smothered rage, he faced the Greek, gave him his I.D. card, and said, "Get out of here!"

The Greek smiled, waved, and buzzed away into the darkness from which he came. Rich asked, "Shouldn't we have kept him?"

Guy answered curtly, "Yep."

"Won't we get into trouble?"

"I will, not you."

"So why'd you let him go?"

"Because I'm going to take a fall, but Schlumberger is coming with me. I'm going to nail that jerk, even if I get court-martialed."

"You'd cut off your nose to spite your own face?"

"To get Schlumberger? Yes, that's exactly what I'm doing. I've *had* it with him. He could've cost us our lives."

Guy waited impatiently to get off duty. Someone must have heard the radio broadcasts and he wanted a confrontation. To solidify his position, he made a radio check every hour and, not surprisingly, Schlumberger replied that he read him "loud and clear." When he was relieved, Guy ran to the gunroom. He handed in his weapons and looked for Schlumberger. Contrary to his usual behavior, Schlumberger didn't report to the back office that morning. He quickly left as soon as he could. Guy didn't report the incident and neither did Frank.

A month later, however, Guy received some interesting news about the incident from the adjacent Greek airbase. A Greek guard told a Greek American who in turn told Guy that the intruder claimed to have been fired upon with submachine guns. Thankfully, no reporters interviewed such a "reliable" source.

At Christmas, Frank Schlumberger was due to rotate back to "the world." He no longer pulled duty and was to catch his flight home the day after the security police Christmas party. He walked into the barely lit, crowded Christmas party and met the hostile looks of his compatriots with an ingenuous smile. In civilian clothes, he looked even more like a boy than he did in uniform. Guy nodded hello to him and wished he'd pick a fight with him or, better yet, with Liberty, just to show how "tough" he was.

A couple of minutes later, Vlad Pettenkoffer, who tended to be innocuous on nearly all occasions, surprised Guy by saying, "A bunch of us are going to jump that creep!" His head nodded toward Frank. "Are you in?"

Guy asked, "Just the non-lifers?"

"Both lifers and non-lifers! Are you in?"

"Yeah, I'm in."

Five minutes later, Vlad ran up to Guy and said, "Damn it! He got away! Someone must have tipped him off!"

Guy said, "Maybe not. He must know how we all feel about him. I haven't seen him all week and, hopefully, this is the last time I'll ever see him – for eternity! I'm glad he's gone."

No one ever saw Schlumberger again. He slipped back into the United States on a flight no one bothered to see off.

THE CAPER OF THE MISSING SEDAN

From the moment Tech Sergeant Thomas Whittle and Airman Claudius Boatman, met at Athenai Airbase, they hated one another. Whittle was a fat-bellied, ex-sheriff from Alabama with all the vices and virtues of that species of mankind. He was intelligent, crafty, and tough, and adhered to the good-old-boy system of the South. Honor was important, violence was accepted, and a man had to be a man, however that was defined.

Boatman, on the other hand, was tall, slender, and hard. He was well-educated simply because he was well-read. He was another breed found commonly in the Air Force: the disillusioned college dropout. Like Cato of ancient Rome, he was a good hater. To all appearances, he was a cultured New Englander from solid Yankee stock. In fact, he was the son of an overworked, underpaid mill worker. Boatman was at war with the world, and his small, gray, expressionless eyes were evidence of this.

The trouble started after Boatman had been transferred to Whittle's flight, which pulled duty from 2300 hours at night to 0700 hours in the morning. As usual, just before guard mount, Liberty had gone into the gun room to be issued his .38 Special and eighteen rounds of ammunition. He gave Whittle his gun card, which was to be exchanged for his weapon.

Turning on his heels, Whittle led the way into the small, ironclad room lined with M-16s and metal boxes full of cartridges. As the sergeant pretended to look for a weapon, he managed to get between Liberty and the gray metal door leading out of the room. Then Whittle dropped all pretenses and started to shoulder Boatman. When the airman shifted to let the sergeant pass, Whittle still stepped into him.

Two hundred and fifty pounds of brawn pushed Liberty into a corner. Quickly, the airman calculated his chances should he take the bait and strike Whittle. There was too little space for him to use his long arms and legs effectively, and Whittle outweighed him by at least fifty pounds. The sergeant would kill him. He tolerated the subtle abuse until Whittle realized his efforts to provoke a fight had failed.

After Liberty was issued his weapon, he loaded it at the gun barrel, holstered it, and then proceeded to guard mount, which was held beneath the one light before the police station. The tour of duty in Greece was two and a half years. That was plenty of time to get Whittle back.

During the next month, things hadn't improved. Liberty did everything he could safely do to annoy Whittle. He kept his hands in his pockets and slouched against walls instead of standing up sharply in military fashion. He always addressed Whittle as Sarrrge, prolonging the "r" sound because Whittle showed how much it annoyed him.

One night at guard mount, Whittle said, "Boatman, you look like a razorback gone hippie! Didn't I tell you to get a haircut?"

Liberty hung his head down and replied, "Um, I think so, Sarrrge." He opened his mouth slightly because he knew it made him look simple.

Whittle rocked back and forth, controlling his anger and frustration. His arms jerked spastically as he fought his inclination to hit the airman. Whittle said, "You look like you been dancing in a hog wallow! Ain't you ashamed of yourself? When was the last time you shined your shoes?"

With Whittle's needle-like eyes piercing him, Liberty murmured, "I don't know, Sarrrge."

"By guard mount tomorrow, I want you to have a haircut ... a real haircut, not greased down like you did last week to make it look short. I also want you to shine your shoes so I can see myself good enough to shave. You got that?"

"Sure, Sarrrge."

Whittle took one step down the row of military policemen. He faced Pete, another young cop and Liberty's friend. Shaking his head in a deprecating manner, Whittle said, "Wallich, you got some partner there!" Almost like an afterthought, he gritted his teeth and his jaw tightened. He spit out, "He's a damned idiot!"

After briefly inspecting the troops, Whittle read the announcements. He said, "Men, be careful. A Greek cop was blown up today. He spotted a brown paper bag beneath a monument. When he opened the bag, it exploded and killed him. It was probably the work of Greek nationalists. If you see any packages, especially on the flight line, call it in and we'll get the bomb squad to you. If you see something unusual, call for backup."

Whittle rattled off the post assignments, "Wallich, you got main gate, Siebold, flight line, Finkbinder desk, Airman Victor, flight line with Siebold." He faced Liberty. "You've got base patrol. Use the six-pack and take Yiorgos with you. Any questions? Good. Attention, dismissed."

Liberty, with Yiorgos in tow, hopped into the pickup truck. After adjusting the mirror so he couldn't see himself, he pulled out of the parking lot and headed into the dark.

Every shift had a Greek interpreter and Yiorgos worked the night shift. He was Boatman's age, but in every other respect was his opposite. Yiorgos was short, dark, expressive, and happy. His large brown eyes danced with joy. There was a lively spring in his walk and usually a bright smile was bursting from beneath his thick mustache. He was as alert and curious as a ferret.

Despite his jovial openness, he had more than his share of trouble. Living in an impoverished country with poor health programs, he took care of an ailing mother as a good Greek son should do. During the day he worked as a travel agent and during the night he worked for the U.S. Air Force. Somewhere in between, he found time for sleep. Already, he spoke four languages fluently.

The base was surrounded by a series of dirt roads down which Liberty liked to drive. Although dry and dusty, they still reminded him of dairy farms and fishing trips. Now, Liberty drove down one of those roads, passed a stacked pile of telephone poles, and stopped before a bare field full of huge potholes.

As he sat behind the steering wheel, idling the engine, he said, "Do you know that I grew up next to a dairy farm? My mother wrote to me and told me that the whole thing was sold, flattened, and houses put there instead. You see, D equals D. Development equals death. Developers destroy everything first before they build. Nothing was left of the farm, not even the stone walls. Sometimes I get overwhelmed by a sense of futility. There's the Vietnam War, the protestors, the draft dodgers, and I thoroughly hate Congress. ... I feel so empty."

Abruptly, Liberty gunned the engine of the truck and shifted it into first gear. He asked, "Do you think we can make it across?"

Yiorgos answered, without a trace of accent, "Liberty, I do not think so. We will break an axle."

"Then we break an axle."

Because it was night, the potholes looked huge and black as though they touched the bowels of the earth. The Greek fastened his seat belt as the sinister field awaited them. Boatman said, "Well, here goes."

He hit the accelerator. Shifting from first into second gear, he zigzagged wildly in his efforts to avoid the potholes, but there were so many that he was forced to run through them. The truck rocked back and forth, up and down. Sometimes they saw the black of the sky with the headlights lost in its immensity, nearly overwhelming Liberty with its futility. Sometimes they saw the pale brown earth that caught the glow of the headlights in two small, tight, round balls. Liberty gritted his teeth and yelled, "YEEEEE-HHHAAAAAA!"

Three minutes later, they were across. Liberty stopped the truck and let the swirl of dust catch up to them. He triumphed, "We made it!" He could see that Yiorgos, although laughing, was upset. Liberty waited for the excitement to settle. He asked, "Shall we try it again?"

Yiorgos jumped. "No, let us not. Too much excitement is not a good thing. I want to enjoy the moment. Another try would ruin it."

Boatman asked, "Do you really think we've done enough?"

"Yes, I do."

"You realize that we made history. You'll be able to tell your great-grandchildren about this."

Yiorgos affirmed, "And I will tell them. This moment will live for as long as men breathe."

"Good."

Liberty slammed the truck into gear and swung around by the Washeteria where the young wives did their laundry. Leaving the truck, Liberty walked through the two rooms housing the rows of washing machines and dryers.

He stopped and caught his breath. Bending over a dryer was Clara. She wore a tight tee shirt that accentuated her small breasts and tight shorts that accentuated her full, long legs. When she straightened, her pallid blue eyes met Liberty's eyes. Both seemed to flash. He noticed her fine sand-colored hair that framed the healthy bronze tan of her face. They exchanged hellos and he casually continued his rounds.

As soon as he was out the door, he ran to Yiorgos' window. He asked, "What time is it?"

"Almost midnight."

Liberty said pensively, "Damn! I won't have time to do a laundry before post change."

"Didn't you do a laundry last night?"

"Yeah, but that was because Linda was here."

"Your clothes must be clean then."

"Yes, but that doesn't matter. They were clean last night, too. The important thing is to do a laundry." He whined, "Yiorgos, I'm in love. She's gorgeous. You should see her legs! Believe me, this is the chance of a lifetime!"

"Why don't you just go in and talk to her?"

"I can't. I don't have that kind of guts. What if I propositioned her and she turned me down? I've got to make it look natural, like I'm there for a reason. Yiorgos, think of something!"

A few minutes later, a shooting star dashed across the sky and faded toward the earth. Neither man could think of a good reason for Liberty to go inside to talk with Clara. He could have made something up, but it would have sounded like a lie and he didn't want to be too obvious. Finally, with a sad shake of his head, Liberty rejoined Yiorgos in the truck.

As the truck started into motion, the interpreter mumbled. Liberty asked, "What?"

Yiorgos said, "Is not that what you Americans say, never a dull moment?"

The Crossroads, the base cafeteria, was closed, but the snack bar at the flight line was open. Liberty, despondent over his latest failure, drove there to buy a BLT and a coffee. Having securely jammed them between the windshield and dashboard so they wouldn't fall, he drove along another dirt road until he found a convenient stopping place. By chance, he parked near the transmitting installation called by the cops the radio shack.

The truck in which the two men sat was called a six-pack because it had two rows of seats, enough for six men. Yiorgos, who wasn't hungry, wanted to sleep. Liberty offered, "You can rack out in

the back if you want. After I eat, I'm going to do some reading before post change." Yiorgos crawled into the back seat and fell asleep
within seconds.

Boatman ate his lunch in the dark. The truck was facing a re-
cently painted, silver chain-link fence that separated the Greek airbase from the American airbase. A few tufts of grass spotted the
mostly bare, yellow soil characteristic of the area.

In his rearview and side mirrors, he could see the well-
lighted area of the radio complex. It was surrounded by a ten-foot-
tall chain-link fence, topped by razor wire. The building's drab green
sideboards and peaked, tiled roof made it look like a garage. Only
the tall metal-framed tower, an excellent imitation of a child's erec-
tor set, belied that impression.

Boatman noticed the sweep of headlights and heard a car
behind him. He heard a car door slam and watched in his rearview
mirror as a senior sergeant, a striper, entered the complex. Two
minutes later he heard Finkbinder's voice over the car radio, "Control to Car Four."

He picked up his mike and keyed it. "Four by."

"Be advised that we received a call from the shack. There's
an unidentified Air Force sedan parked near them. It's between them
and the Greek airbase. Check it out."

Liberty took a quick look about him. He realized, since his
was the only vehicle in the area, that his truck was the unidentified
car. He didn't know why they called it in as a sedan instead of a
pickup truck, but he was certain Finkbinder was talking about him.
He didn't want to admit that he had stopped here to eat, since that
would be interpreted to mean that he was goofing off. He called
back and said, melodramatically, "Control, I'm on my way."

He ate half his sandwich, then he keyed the mike. "Control,
this is Car Four. I'm at the radio shack. I don't see any cars here other than the private cars of the GIs working here." For effect he added, "I must have scared him off."

Pleased with the way he had handled the situation, Liberty
returned the mike to its receiver. He heard the shack door open and

53

close and watched in his mirrors as the striper walked toward him. Liberty thought about waking Yiorgos but he decided to let him sleep.

When the striper reached the truck, he asked belligerently, "What are you doing here?"

Liberty asked just as belligerently, "Who are *you*?"

"I'm the NCO who runs the shack."

Liberty imitated Gomer Pyle. "Gollly. Well, *I'm* impressed."

"Okay, wise ass, what are you doing here?"

Liberty held up his sandwich. "What does it look like?"

Liberty could see the rows of stripes on the sergeant's shoulders. He knew that the man was standing so that he could see them at eye level. He also knew that this was meant to intimidate him.

The striper asked, deep anger edging his voice, "Why are you eating *here*?"

Liberty answered just as sharply, "Because I *want* to eat here."

The striper clenched his fists and gritted his teeth. He walked to the front of the truck, then back toward Liberty. It was obvious that the striper wanted to rip the truck apart, bolt by bolt, and pile it on the mutilated corpses of its occupants.

Boatman expected to be assaulted and wondered if he should get out of the truck to give himself more room. He didn't want to be trapped in the cab with this man pounding him in the head. He thought, *I can always jam the truck door into him. That'll give me the break I need.* He decided to wait for the event. If there was a fight, then there was a fight, but he would not back down, sergeant or no sergeant.

The striper stopped at his window and growled, "This is a restricted area; you're not supposed to be here."

Liberty was about to imitate Gomer Pyle again, but decided that it would be too incendiary. Instead, he snapped, "Fine. When I'm done eating, I'll move."

The striper jumped as though he'd stepped on a snake. Boatman was pleased that he had scored such an obvious point. It was then that he heard the crunching of gravel. Again looking into his mirrors, he saw two more airmen coming from the radio shack.

Like a pacing lion, the striper walked to the front of the truck again. He was pretty stout, but Liberty thought he might be able to dispatch him quickly with a punch into his throat. That would leave the other two, but they didn't look nearly as formidable as the striper. He wasn't sure, but he thought he could pull it off. At any rate, he would not back down.

When the striper returned, he paused at Liberty's window. Somewhere in the back of his mind, the striper had reviewed all of his alternatives. None of them looked good. He badly wanted to say something to Boatman, but his anger, furiously intense, kept him from uttering a sound. He walked quietly away, head bowed, unable to answer the queries of his comrades.

Liberty watched them depart in his rearview mirror. He released a string of expletives in a cascade of rage. He was so angry that he shook uncontrollably.

During this event, Yiorgos had sat up in the back seat and, in a semiconscious daze, watched the activity. he quietly considered his partner, then said, "Liberty, if you are not careful, you will someday kill someone." He then lay down to nap some more.

Barely a minute passed when Liberty heard Whittle's deep, Southern drawl over the radio. "Car Two to Control."

"Control by."

"Call the main gate and tell them not to let any vehicles off-base without notifying me first. Car Three."

"Three by."

"Go to the base ops snack bar and check it out for any Air Force sedans."

"Ten four."

"Car Four."

Liberty answered, "Four by."

"Go to the base commander's office and see if you can find any Air Force sedans."

"Ten four."

Yiorgos, who had been listening, moved from the back to the front seat. He said, "Liberty, they are talking about us."

"I know. I wonder why the shack called us in as a sedan."

"It is dark. Maybe we looked like a sedan."

Liberty put the truck into gear and headed for Main Base Road. He saw a police car race down base and didn't recognize the driver. He asked, "Who's that?"

Yiorgos shrugged.

They heard Whittle's voice over the radio. "Control, this is Car Two. Have the main gate put the chain up. Car Five."

"Five by." Listening carefully, Liberty tried to recognize the new voice.

"Go to The Crossroads and check it out."

"Ten four."

Liberty saw another police car race down base. Turning toward Yiorgos he asked, "Who's Car Five?"

"Beats me."

A few more calls over the radio brought a new, alarming thought to Liberty. His eyes widened and he said, "Shit! They're having a recall and *I'm* the man they're after!" Closing his eyes, he whined, "Aw, *man*! I've got to stop this right now or every off-duty cop will be in here humping planes all night because of *me*!" He rolled his head in agony as he continued, "I've got to confess to Whittle. He already thinks I'm a raving idiot and now he's got proof. Worst of all, the other guys will think I'm a jerk, too! I can't handle confession. There must a way out. I need to think."

Before they had time to follow through, they saw Whittle coming toward them from the opposite direction. Liberty stopped his truck when Whittle was about to pass him. He waved his left arm out the window and Whittle pulled up next to him. The sergeant asked, "What is it, Boatman?"

Liberty hesitated, then he swallowed his pride. Like a penitent, he said, "Sarrrge, I've solved the case of the missing sedan."

"Who is it?"

"I'm not sure, but, um, I think it's me."

Whittle took a deep breath as his hands curled, white-knuckled, about the steering wheel. Taking short, sharp breaths, Whittle eventually calmed himself enough to say, "Boatman, I almost called a recall because of you! I even made a report to the base commander!" Whittle waited a full minute before asking, "What were you doing outside the shack?"

"Eating."

"Did anybody see you?"

"Yeah, a striper and a couple of his pals."

"What'd you tell them?"

"Same's I told you, Sarge."

Whittle exploded like a fragment grenade. "Why'd you do a stupid thing like that? First of all, you shouldn't be eating lunch in a restricted area! Any dope knows that! Secondly, if you get caught doing something stupid, you lie. Got that? You should have said that you thought you saw a Greek climbing the fence."

"But Sarrrrge, I *didn't* see a Greek climbing the fence."

Rocking back and forth, Whittle yelled, "Cut out the crap!" Every nerve in his body begged him to kill this airman. Another long minute passed. Whittle's body suddenly slumped. Pathetically, he said, "Never mind, Boatman, just never mind."

After Whittle slammed his car into gear and drove away, Yiorgos clapped his hands. He laughed, "Bravo, Liberty, bravo."

Liberty's eyes twinkled and the straight line of his mouth lengthened ever so slightly.

The next morning, Wallich and Liberty walked back to the barracks. They went directly to Wallich's room where they could sit and wind down from the night's activity. While they waited for exhaustion to catch up with them, Liberty told Pete the story of the missing sedan.

Pete laughed and Liberty said, "I know it's funny now, but at the time it wasn't so funny. I could've gotten into some really serious trouble, and then I had to humiliate myself to Whittle. You know, I made my voice sound real weak when I talked with him, kind of in a fawning way."

Just then, they heard a knock on Boatman's door. Liberty asked, "Who could that be?" He opened Pete's door a crack and looked toward his room. He saw Whittle. In total surprise, Liberty opened Pete's door further.

Whittle saw him and said, "Oh, there you are. That was quite a scene last night. About a year ago, we actually did chase a Greek the length of that fence. He was a soldier and he was carrying a sack on his back that must have weighed eighty pounds. I didn't think a man could run that fast with all that weight on his back. Anyway, the reason why I came here is to tell you that I spoke to the base commander and squared everything away. You have nothing to worry about."

Liberty answered, "Good enough. Thanks, Sarge."

"Sure thing."

As they listened to Whittle walk down the corridor, Liberty faced Pete. He shrugged and said defensively, "It's not *my* fault. I didn't ask him to see the base commander."

THE HOSTAGES

Bob Siebold was a tall, strong Midwesterner whose Nordic ancestry was adequately demonstrated by his square, firm jaw set beneath clear, deep blue eyes. Like Liberty, he was hard and efficient, but he lacked his friend's fierce hostility, his hatred of the world.

Bob was a particular problem for Liberty, who didn't believe anyone was fearless; yet, that is exactly what Bob seemed to be. Frequently, during their three-day breaks, the two friends visited the ruins like those at Delphi and Corinth, places where huge boulders and tall cliffs sprouted from the barren soil. Always, these treks involved side expeditions of rock climbing. Bob would find a cliff and ask, excitement adding a rich mellow tone to his voice, "Want to climb it?"

Liberty would feel the challenge. His eyes would scan the cliff face, looking for comfortable ledges and bushes which might break his fall should he, indeed, fall. The higher he looked up, the lower his heart sank, but just as he never backed down from a fight, he wouldn't back down here, either. With a barely heard grumble, he'd say, "Might as well." Then he'd follow Bob's lead.

During the climb, Liberty would look straight into the rock before him. To look either up or down was too much like looking into the incomprehensible, coldly unforgiving face of eternity. Bob, on the other hand, would be leaping up as freshly unconcerned as if he were a mountain goat on a well-worn trail.

When not climbing cliffs, the two went swimming along the cliff-lined shores. The water would be at least thirty feet deep two feet from where the rocks first kissed the water. In a magnificent dive, Bob would plunge into the Aegean Sea from a forty-foot cliff. Whenever Liberty witnessed it, his heart leapt to his throat, thus strangling the scream trying to force its way through.

Often, after a handful of dives, Bob would ask, "How close am I coming to the rocks?"

Liberty would look carefully at Bob to see if he was joking; then he would ask in turn, "Did it ever occur to you to consider that question *before* your first dive?"

Despite his own fear, Liberty did not think himself a coward. Admittedly, the diving was a bit much for him, but on more than one occasion, he faced down gangs of bad guys, namely, American sailors out to waste their money.

One day, to the surprise of both of them, they were ordered on to the day shift to pull flight line duty together. To Whittle, this seemed like the most logical choice. He and the other airmen were told that an Italian airliner had been hijacked and had landed at Athenai Airport. Three terrorists held fourteen hostages in an attempt to free three other terrorists already in a Greek prison. Liberty and Siebold were to keep the terrorists from accessing the American airbase. Both men were the best shots among the security police. Siebold was clear-headed and his courage was never in question. Liberty was nearly uncontrollably violent. Whittle silently prayed, *Oh please, oh please, oh please let Boatman get these guys!*

In addition to their .38 Specials, they were issued M-16s. They were about to get into the blue Ford pickup when Whittle stopped them. He grabbed Liberty's arm and pulled him forcefully to one side. He whispered, "If you take a prisoner, I want you to find an excuse and kill him. Otherwise, the politicians will play their games and more people will get hurt. Remember when the French were blackmailed into letting that terrorist guy go?" Liberty nodded his head yes and remembered how outraged he had been. "Don't let that happen here. You'll be down there the whole eight-hour shift." Liberty nodded his head again.

When he joined Bob in the pickup, his friend asked, "What was that all about?"

Liberty shrugged his shoulders and said, "Nothing really." Then he added, "I hate to say it, but I'm starting to like that guy."

On the way to the flight line, they stopped at the Base Ops snack bar for the coffees they'd nurse for the next eight hours. They pulled up to the pickup that was already blocking the entrance ramp from the runway to the U.S. Air Force flight line. They exchanged brief greetings with the airmen they were relieving. Now, their own truck would be blocking the flight line.

Liberty and Siebold took off their white caps, got out of the truck, and scanned the aircraft with passionless eyes. Less than fifty yards away sat a 707 with its cargo of terror. Liberty mentally calculated the size a head would be from that distance and knew he could make the shot, even if a hostage was used as a screen. Unlike Siebold and Whittle, both of whom had served in Vietnam, he had never killed a man and vaguely wondered how it would feel.

Siebold cocked his head to one side and said, as if reminiscing, "It kind of reminds me of Jonah and the whale." He looked at the 707, then at the surrounding flat surfaces of cement cut by rows of scraggly bushes and drought-starved grass. "I guess we're the only ones down here. I don't even see the wild dogs. Where are our Hollywood heroes when we need them?"

In a quick, violent movement, Liberty turned and faced the large square building of Base Operations that sat behind them. Cupping his hands to his mouth, he yelled with all the bitterness consuming him, "Hey, where's our backup, you mothers?! Here! This is what I think of you!" Making a fist with his right hand, he swung it up as his left hand caught the arm at the elbow in an obscene gesture. He yelled, "Here! That's for you!"

He heard Bob laughing, a subtle rumble of distant thunder. Between chuckles, he said, "They probably saw you."

Liberty felt sudden relief. He said, "Good. I hope they did. It's just that I get so tired of everything. We're in a war that we're expected to win and not win. To get back at Nixon, the Arabs threaten to blow us up once a week and here I am sitting beneath a boiling sun on a scorching flight line in the middle of nowhere wondering if I'm going to be killed by some wandering nomad. Something's wrong."

By now, the mood was totally relaxed. They could have been sitting in a lounge telling stories. Siebold said, "I was in Vietnam during the Tet offensive. We would have been overrun but the Viet Cong attacked during post change, so there were twice as many armed cops as normal. We won that battle. The news was wrong. I was there. I don't get why the media is always bad-mouthing us and making our victories into defeat. I don't get it. Is it Russian psyops? Ivy League Marxism? I don't get it." He paused and then continued. "Before Tet the cops were treated like second-class citizens by the people on base. After we saved their asses, they couldn't do enough for us."

Liberty said, "I know one thing. We're not going to get attacked," he tossed his chin in the direction of the 707, "by those guys."

"How do you know?"

"Haven't you noticed? Terrorists never attack armed men. They don't have the guts."

Bob was skeptical. "Sounds like famous last words to me. What about suicide bombers?"

"It's easy to die, especially if you're nuts. It's living that's hard. Pity those suckers back home who build roads and lay sewer lines and make shirts and soda and all that other junk ... and raise families to boot. They're the real heroes. I don't think I could do any of that crap."

Throughout the day, the men talked of women and of former deployments, favorite subjects of the GIs. Bob said, "Once I was on leave in Danang. It was the craziest thing I ever saw. Suddenly I heard a popping noise and bullets started whinging all over the place. I crawled beneath a truck and hid. It was a gunfight between Black and white GIs. When it was over, about five or six GIs got killed on both sides. I tell people that Br'er Rabbit no longer wears blue jeans. Today he wears fatigues and carries an M-16."

Liberty said, "I think the craziest thing I ever heard was about Korea. It wasn't a racial thing. What happened is that the GIs, both Black and white, would shack up with Korean girls during their tours of duty. The problem is that the girls would fall in love with the GIs. More than once a girl cut off a GI's dick while he was sleeping, then committed suicide herself. She couldn't stand the idea of his leaving her when his tour of duty was over."

His tone of voice became confidential. "Wallich said that he was on main gate one night when a GI ran up with blood streaming down his trousers." He paused. A puzzled look came into his hard, gray eyes. "You know what got me? Wallich said that he put his pants on. These guys would be bleeding to death and each and every one of them would put his pants on. You'd think they wouldn't bother."

Hour edged into hour and story followed story. Liberty couldn't remember the last time he had so much fun. All the while, the 707 stared blindly at them from its multi-windowed eyes. Toward the end of the shift, Bob asked, "Have you seen Vlad's wife?"

Confused, Liberty asked, "Blad?"

"Vlad Pettenkoffer's wife. She arrived yesterday. You won't even believe her body. She reminds me of the front end of a '57 Chevy."

"What do you mean?"

"She's built like a brick shithouse."

"Well, that certainly clarifies it." As an image with large breasts, voluptuous hips and long, smooth legs was forming in Liberty's mind, he suddenly felt as though he was being watched. Huge, sightless eyes were boring down on him. He started and faced the aircraft. He said, "It just occurred to me that while you and I are joking and laughing and telling stories, fourteen people have been in abject terror not fifty yards away. I haven't thought of them once all day."

Both men paused in thought and looked at the 707. A minute passed, then Siebold asked, "Did I tell you about the ambush we had set up in Vietnam?" The stories recommenced.

The next day, Liberty got out of his bunk, showered, and walked to the cafeteria for breakfast. He joined a table of off-duty policemen. Bob was already there. As Liberty sat down with his tray of scrambled eggs and home fries, he heard Bob say, "Nothing happened on our shift. She sat there like a sulking child. Does anyone know what happened?"

Finkbinder said, "The aircraft is gone."

Siebold asked, "What about the terrorists?"

Finkbinder shrugged and another airman said, "I think the Greeks got them."

Liberty interrupted, "Does anyone actually *know* what happened out there?"

No one could give them a definitive answer and neither he nor Bob ever bothered to find out.

HEINTZ

Guy Burrows and Yiorgos wove their way through the narrow, crooked streets of Athens. Ken Tyler had been involved in a car accident and a report had to be filed. They arrived at the Greek police station where they found Ken sitting quietly in a chair that seemed too small and fragile to support his huge frame. Ken seemed to be pleasantly musing to himself, so after greeting each other, Guy said, "You don't look worried."

Ken responded, "Why should I be? I was stopped on my side of the road. *He* ran into *me*."

"Yeah, well, this is Greece."

Guy sat next to his friend as they watched Yiorgos talking to the police. Then Yiorgos approached them and said to Ken, "They want you to take the blame for the accident. They want you to state that you ran into the Greek. You have insurance; he doesn't. Your insurance will pay for everything."

Ken stated flatly, "I'm not taking the blame for anything."

Yiorgos turned toward Guy and said, "We'll be here for a while. I'm going to get statements and the police report. I'll be in the next room if you need me."

After the interpreter left, Ken said, "The Greek was on a motorcycle coming towards me on the opposite side when he lost control. I stopped my car and waited. He smashed right into me. There's a piece of his leg underneath my car. Do you want to see it?"

Guy said, "No, thanks."

Ken urged his friend, "Yeah, go ahead. Take a look at it."

"No, that's all right. I don't want to see it."

"It's cool, Guy. Check it out."

"I don't know."

"Yeah, man, take a look!"

Guy sighed and left Ken to take a look beneath the car. He stood before the fender that had a fierce gash in it. As he hesitated, he ran his hand along the top of the fender leaving a clear streak in the dust that covered the car and everything else in Greece. He thought, "From dust to dust."

Then he bent and looked into the gash. He saw a strip of meat a foot and a half long, three inches wide, and an inch thick. Globs of yellow fat hung to the dark red meat. Bees and flies were crawling all over it.

Guy straightened himself and swooned. He felt the blood rushing from his head and knew that he was deathly white. Slowly, he tottered into the police station and rejoined Ken in the waiting room. His friend said, "Looks like a big slab of beef jerky, don't it?"

Guy nodded yes and said, "That Greek must be horribly hurt."

Ken said pleasantly, "Naw, it wasn't so bad. That's mostly meat you saw. No major arteries were hit nor any important organs. He'll be all right."

As Guy sat there, a deathly shade of pale, he watched the Greek police come to the waiting room door to look at him. He could hear them in the next room talking about him and laughing.

Soon, Yiorgos was ready to leave. Ken stayed behind to fill out more forms. As Guy and Yiorgos were leaving, two Greek policemen got on either side of Guy and were about to hold him up by his arms as if he was an invalid. They were laughing and Guy said, in Greek, "No, no, thank you very much." He forced himself to smile to let them know that he was in on the joke and that he wasn't offended.

When they arrived back on base, the guard mount for the oncoming flight had already taken place and Guy was relieved of duty. He immediately went to The Crossroads for breakfast and to wind down and was surprised to find Liberty there. He told Liberty the story and added, "It was like looking at myself, like when you look at the goat heads in the butcher shops, or some slaughtered goats in a field. I couldn't help but see myself as a piece of meat and that's all. I mean, that's what we are, pieces of meat! We're hideous beneath this covering of skin!"

Liberty agreed, "It's like having reality thrust into your face and what's harder to deal with than reality?"

A couple of days later, Guy was transferred, temporarily, to the day shift. Arab terrorists were threatening the base yet again, so the flight personnel were being realigned to deal with it. As far as Guy was concerned, it was just one more reason to hate terrorists. The good part was that he could get a good night's sleep instead of sleeping in sweat-drenched sheets during the day.

He was tired, unusually so. After work he decided to take a nap before going to The Crossroads for supper. As he was sleeping, he was partially awakened by the sound of someone in his room. Like all GIs, Guy kept everything locked at all times and knew no one could get into his room without waking him. Yet, there was someone in his room.

He sat up and found a tall, platinum-blond man standing next to his bed. He wore a khaki uniform with no insignia. He stood with his arms crossed and stared down at him. Guy looked away and thought, *this man isn't real. I'm dreaming.* He looked again at the blond man and noted the light blue eyes and sharp, angular features. Again, Guy looked away. He picked up his pillow and thought, *if I throw this at him, that's a conscious act and I'll know I'm awake.*

Guy faced his guest and threw the pillow. He watched as the pillow went through the young man, who still stood commandingly before him. Guy thought, *stay calm and talk to him.* He opened his mouth, fully meaning to remain civil, but instead screamed at the top of his lungs and lunged for the door. Chains, bolts, locks, vaults, nothing could have kept him in that room. In two seconds, he was pounding on Pete Wallich's door. "Pete! Pete! Let me in! For God's sake, let me in!"

The door opened and Guy was in the safety of another man's presence. For the second time that week he was ivory-white. He sat in Pete's lounge chair, exhausted as though he'd run ten miles. When he collected himself, he said, "Pete, you'll never believe what just happened."

Pete said, "Whatever it is, you're white as a sheet."

"I think I saw a ghost, an actual ghost."

"I don't know if you saw a ghost, but you definitely saw something, or thought you saw something."

"He was as real to me as you are right now."

Pete reasoned, "It's not drugs since you don't take drugs. It can't be a flashback since you've never taken acid. I would think it's due to stress."

"I don't care what you think it is. Not every mystical experience can be attributed to drugs or psychosis. I'm telling you that I saw a ghost, a spirit if you'd like. It was as real to me as you are now."

"How do you know you weren't dreaming?"

"Because I threw my pillow at him and that's a conscious act. If I really did throw my pillow, then I was awake and he was real."

"Let's take a look."

They went into Guy's room and found that he had really thrown his pillow. Pete said, "It still doesn't mean he was real. Once

68

on guard duty in Korea, I thought I saw a ten-foot soccer ball bounce across a field to me. I stood next to it all night and it sat there with me. I was wide awake and there it was, but I still don't think it was real."

Guy said, "At any rate, he was a German." Then he added jokingly, "I think his name was Heintz."

Pete asked, "Did you know that this base was occupied by the Germans during World War II? Maybe he's one of them."

"Maybe." It suddenly occurred to Guy that he still had to live in that room. Night was coming upon them and he'd have to face Heintz alone, in the dark. He said, "Pete, can you do me a favor?"

"Sure."

"If you hear any screaming or if I call you, can you come over right away?"

"Sure."

Guy didn't admit it to anyone, but he started sleeping with his lights on. This continued until he fell asleep one afternoon. His lights were off since it had been daylight when he dozed off. When he awoke in the late evening, it was pitch black. His first thought was, *Heintz turned the lights off!* That meant that Heintz was in the room watching him.

Guy broke into a cold sweat. He was afraid to move for fear of bumping into Heintz. Wrapped in a fetal position, he started screaming, "Pete, help me! Pete! Pete! Help me!"

Pete called from the other side of the wall that separated their rooms, "What's the matter?"

His friend's voice snapped him out of his fear. He answered, "Nothing. I'm okay." He then decided that it was cowardly to sleep with his lights on. From that moment on, he slept with them bravely turned off. He never saw Heintz again.

Pete asked, the next time they met, "How are you doing?"

Guy answered, "Fine."

"And how is Heintz?"

"Gone, I hope." Then he added, "Heintz taught me one thing. He taught me that there might well be a spirit world, that we're not just pieces of meat."

"It sounds like wishful thinking to me."

"It might be. I don't know if he was real or not, but I sure as hell hope so."

LARRY BUBB

Iiberty was angry. He was forced to sit through race relations classes. He steamed as he listened to how the establishment painted its missiles white to indicate white supremacy, that Pushkin was a great writer because he was one-eighth Black, and that Napoleon lost at Waterloo because an African tribe had kept his men from getting salted meat.

For Liberty, the tone of the class had been set from the very first day. The class was run by two Black instructors. The first, Christopher Dean, was a heavy-set man who literally glowed with health and intelligence. He was more of a guide for the other instructor, John Mello, who conducted the actual course. Although Mello tried to be fair, his racial biases kept sliding out of hiding. One day he asked, "Does anyone know of any cases of reverse discrimination?"

Liberty raised his hand and was about to speak when Mello said curtly, "This isn't high school; you don't have to raise your hand."

After the rebuttal, Liberty said, "*Time* magazine has an article on the Bakke case."

With barely concealed contempt, Mello said, "It wasn't in *Time*. It was in *Newsweek*!" In fact, it was in both magazines, but Liberty got the message. Mello went on to inform the class that the Bakke case was one small injustice to one white man while the whole Black race was and is victimized by discrimination.

The class was composed of twenty men, fifteen whites and five Blacks. Fortunately, they were predominately good people and liked one another so they managed to avoid the fistfights that sometimes broke out in other classes.

The main reason Liberty hated the class was that its members behaved like cows at a watering trough. No matter how ridiculous Mello's claims were, Liberty could look at the men sitting in the circle and see them all nodding their heads in unison. *Like cows*, Liberty thought, *just like cows*.

Liberty did have one surprise, though. Mello asked short, scrappy, Larry Bubb, a man with a richly comforting dark brown skin, "When you go to the bowling alley and see a white gang standing near the door, how do you feel?"

Larry answered, "I'm a little afraid when I have to walk around them."

Liberty almost asked, "Why?" He had always assumed that white beatings of Black men was media hype and an antiquated world-view where only Black people are beaten and raped, evidenced by outdated films from the 60s. Of the many beatings he knew of personally, including once when he was beaten in D.C., they had all been whites beating on whites, Blacks beating on whites, or Blacks beating on Blacks, but never, not ever, whites beating on Blacks. It seemed to be a literary and media cliché dating from the Jim Crow South and Liberty thought it was a lie, at least in the real world. Yet, here was Larry admitting his fear of white gangs. Bubb wasn't a liar or a coward. If he was afraid, there was a reason for it.

The class ended on Friday. On that day, the twenty men formed an informal group and admitted that Blacks and whites were brothers. They also agreed unanimously, with the exception of Liberty and Mello who saw the irony, that Puerto Ricans were dirty, piled their trash everywhere, and liked to have sex in hallways.

Within a week of his class, racial tensions flared again. This time, a Black, 19-year-old airman named Oakley allegedly committed statutory rape with a white girl. Oakley was court-martialed, and shortly before the verdict, the Blacks, led by Christopher Dean, threatened to riot. Liberty and the rest of the off-duty airmen were recalled. At 1900 hours, he was at guard mount with Bob Siebold, Pete Wallich, and twenty-five other cops. Only four Blacks were there: Tony Frick, Larry Bubb, Bob Body, and Ken Tyler. Whittle was the flight chief. Each man was issued an M-16 in addition to his .38 Special.

Standing before the men formed into two, straight rows, Whittle said, "Men, we have a problem. Militant Blacks have reserved all the tables at the NCO Club. That's not the problem. The problem is that they're letting no one else into the club and they're threatening to tear it apart and burn it down. Gentlemen, I'm not putting up with it."

A wave of excitement passed through the ranks as the cops looked at one another, all of them except the Black airmen, who stared into empty space in front of them. Liberty could only see the backs of their heads as he wondered what they were thinking. The choice of action would be hard for them. His own choice was easy.

They waited at the police station for an hour, waiting for things to come to a head, when the riot was called off. The militants dispersed of their own accord. The issued weapons were returned to the gun room and a possible confrontation was avoided. The cops went home. The following day, Oakley was acquitted and the day after that, he was sent to Germany to finish his tour of duty.

One night, when Liberty was pulling main gate, he watched the hordes of sailors inundating the base like an unwanted, uncontrolled, infestation of rats. He said bitterly to Yiorgos, "Tonight's going to be a long, freaking night."

A taxi stopped in front of the gate and let out seven sailors. Liberty waved them through.

Yiorgos said, "They help Greece. They clean up our streets by marrying our prostitutes."

Soon, Liberty was relieved by Larry Bubb. Pete Wallich pulled up to the gate in the sedan to wait for Liberty to join him on base patrol. As the two bantered with each other, they saw Bob Body and five other militant Black men coming over the small rise before the gate. Bob and Liberty weren't friends, but they weren't enemies either. Whenever they met, they were civil to one another and during the odd times when they shared a post together, they shared their sandwiches and drinks.

When the Black airmen reached the gate, they pointedly talked to Larry and didn't seem to notice Liberty standing there. When Bob looked at him, Liberty said, "Hey, Bob, how's it goin'?" Bob blandly turned away as though Liberty didn't exist. Immediately, Liberty's head snapped back at the mute insult. This had happened often enough with other Black men, but this was the first time with Bob. Liberty bounded from the elevated gate shack, almost knocking the last of the Black men down, opened the car door, then slammed it shut after he sat down. He was enraged. "Those stinking assholes!"

Wallich, always calm and someone who actually believed in the power of reason, asked him patiently, "What do you mean?" In no uncertain terms, Liberty told him exactly what had happened.

Wallich shifted the car into gear and they headed into the night. They drove along the dirt road encircling the base. The soil was so poor that it looked white beneath a brilliant full moon that hung heavily over them. As they bounced slowly along, Wallich said, "You have to understand that Bob is militant."

"So what?"

"Blacks have been oppressed for hundreds of years."

"I haven't oppressed anyone. Why should *I* take the blame for a handful of Southern plantation owners?"

"C'mon. What about the slums?"

"What about them?"

"What would *you* do if you had a family, your child was eating lead paint, and you couldn't find a job?"

"I suppose I'll find out once affirmative action gets done with me!"

"Liberty, I know you well enough to know that if you were treated like a second-class citizen, you'd be in the streets shooting the hell out of everyone."

Liberty thought a moment, slouched in his seat, and finally admitted, "You're right. I wouldn't stand for it, but the fact is that I'm a white man. I don't see Blacks as being weak and helpless or as clever children that I have to condescend to. What's better, to be treated like a clever child or to be treated like a man? Personally, I hope there is a race war so that all these problems can be resolved one way or another and we can all live in peace."

"You don't really believe that, do you?"

"That's what the Greeks would do."

A thin gray fox ran before the headlights of the car and into a culvert. Wallich said, "When I was in Korea there was real racism going on, not like here where the Blacks pretty much do what they want. In Korea, the Blacks were treated badly and I'm not saying that because I'm liberal. Once a buddy and I, the only two whites who'd associate with the Blacks at all, were asked, if there was a race war, who'd we fight for. My buddy hedged and didn't say a word, but I admitted that I'd fight for the Blacks. After that, my name was mud, at least among the whites."

"Pete," Liberty said, "I would have turned against you, too. I mean, you *are* white. You'd be betraying your own people."

"I wanted justice; that's all."

"What's justice? Is it justice that college kids smoke pot all day and get laid every night while you and I rot in Greece? Is it justice when those wooden dildos in Congress play their political games while guys like you and me die in Vietnam? Where's justice? When you find it, you let me know!"

"Well, you'll never find it convincing yourself that it doesn't exist."

"It doesn't exist, or don't you know that yet?"

"You're wrong."

They had gone down one side of the base and were coming up the other side toward the main gate. Liberty said, "I was in D.C. two years ago when they held a Friendship Concert to promote brotherly love. Dozens of white people were beaten, raped and robbed."

"That was an isolated event."

"When something happens dozens of times, it's not an isolated event. When half a dozen white men get beaten by Black gangs, it's not an isolated event."

"Liberty, let me put it this way. At least the Blacks *we* know are in the service with us. They're getting screwed just like you and me. Now, who would you rather have: a white draft dodger or a Black serviceman?"

"You already know the answer to that one."

"Good. Now here's another point I want to make. It's a crime when a nation wastes the talents of its people, white or Black. We can't afford to neglect our best people, white or Black. Am I right?"

They were near the Office of Special Investigations (OSI) building which faced the main gate. Liberty said, "Okay, you made your point, but I still don't understand them. Stop the car; I have to take a leak."

Although there was an outhouse not twenty feet away, Liberty walked to the corner of the OSI building to urinate on it as a symbolic gesture, one that he knew Wallich would appreciate. Instead of urinating, however, he studied the main gate, then leaned casually against the building, crossing his arms and legs, head at a cocky tilt.

Pete noticed the odd behavior and walked up behind him. They watched Larry Bubb as he stood in a wide stance, hands on hips, who in turn watched a group of twenty-five men, nearly all white, strolling up the middle of Main Base Road from the base's bowling alley. The young men were all dressed in casual civilian clothes like those worn by the male models in *Playboy*. Some carried beers while others carried bowling balls. Liberty said over his shoulder, "Navy."

They stopped when they reached Larry, who said, "You men best take them balls back where they belong."

The group's spokesman, a well built, stocky, blond man, said, "We're not taking anything back."

Larry reiterated, "I'm telling you to take them back."

A little to one side of the group stood a sailor who was watching the events unfold as if he wasn't a part of them. His eyes wandered and settled on Liberty and Pete, who had not been noticed by the others. He stared at them for a couple of minutes, was about to warn his friends when Liberty gave him a wickedly bemused Cheshire smile. The sailor walked off quickly, quietly, and alone.

Tension was high as Larry and the spokesman faced one another. The white said, after sweeping his arm toward his followers, "There are twenty-five of us." For emphasis, he pointed at Larry and asked, "What are *you* going to do about it?"

Larry answered, "Oh, *they'll* get by me all right, but *you* won't."

The blond hesitated. He seemed stunned by the possibilities. One look at Bubb convinced him that the Black sergeant meant business. When the words had finally worked their way through the sailor's brain, he turned to his men and said, "Okay, we've had our fun. Let's take them back. Hell, I wanted another beer anyway."

Liberty nodded his approval and said to his partner, "Bubb's quite a man."

As they walked back to the sedan, Pete said, "But he's Black."

Liberty said, "He's different."

"Really? Maybe he's not different to other white men. Maybe, just maybe, Bob Body and Chris Dean are 'different' to *other* white men."

"Okay, Pete, I get it. Let's check to see if he needs anything."

With that, they drove into the lights where Larry could see them. They let him know that they had seen the whole thing and next time, "Damn it, call for backup!"

THE BATH

I had been stationed in Greece as a security guard with the U. S. Air Force for almost three years. It was a soft, quiet kind of duty interspersed with times of great anxiety. I had been two miles away when the forces of the then dictator, Papadopoulous, gunned down several students at Constitution Square in downtown Athens. Witnesses, who I knew personally, said that at least thirty people were killed. The newspapers said nine.

I was a five-minute walk from the carnage created by three Arab terrorists when they threw hand grenades into a crowded waiting area at the civilian airport. They then opened up with automatic weapons. I had even relieved Liberty and Siebold at the flight line when fourteen hostages were being held by yet another group of terrorists.

Now, another crisis was in progress. Another coup had taken place. For three days the base had no contact with the outside world. Several times I tried the police radio in the patrol car and heard the squealing sound of radio waves being jammed by the Greek military.

I loved the Greeks. They were a friendly, smiling people who became violent on only two subjects: soccer and politics. It didn't look good to me that all of our radios were jammed. More often than not, though, I felt like a fly on a battlefield. These things happened around me. I had thus far been only a casual spectator.

It was my day off. By this time, I was living off-base with Pete Wallach. We shared a two-bedroom house set in the middle of a small fig orchard within walking distance of the base.

Wearing a tee shirt, sandals, and cut-offs, I put on my sunglasses and made my way along the quiet, tree-lined streets to the base. Ken Tyler was just going on base patrol and was kind enough to offer me a ride to the cafeteria, The Crossroads, where I hoped to catch up on the latest news. After Ken dropped me off, I got a coffee and a meal of pasticcio and sat at a table dominated by Craig Crofoot.

Tension was running high. Crofoot, a Cherokee Indian, was the center of a small group of young GIs, all of them security guards. I could see by the light glow on his dark face, like that of a happily pregnant woman, that he was bursting with excitement. His thin, lithe body was poised over the others as he stood with one foot on the seat of a chair and leaned toward them.

He asked with a light thrill in his voice, "Have you been listening to the car radio at night? The Greeks are jamming it, just like in the movies! Remember? The GI would be calling base and the Japanese would be jamming his radio!" Craig looked meaningfully at his listeners, his wild, black eyes conveying waves of silent, disturbing messages.

Richard Victor fidgeted. He shifted in his seat. He had been in Greece for almost a month and despite his large, six-foot frame and muscular build, had a wondering, childlike look to his face. He asked, "What do you think the Greeks will do to us?"

Crofoot licked his lips with relish. He said, death and destruction edging his voice, "They could do anything! They shot their own people in Constitution Square. What do you think they'll do to a blond-haired, blue-eyed stranger like you who shouldn't even be here in the first place? Did you see the size of the Greek bayonets?" For emphasis Craig lifted his arms and held his hands two feet apart. "They're at least a foot long!"

I thought Rich was about to pass out, so I interrupted, "Stop scaring everybody. The Greeks aren't going to do anything. They're good people."

Undaunted, Crofoot leaned closer to Richard and asked in a loud whisper, "Do you know what Greek slum clearance is? They block off either end of a street and kill everybody in between."

Rich's mouth visibly dropped and his eyes widened in dismay.

I said, "Rich, don't listen to him. He's only trying to scare you. The Greeks are a nice people. Respect them and they'll respect you."

Rich turned to one of the local heroes and asked, "Liberty, what do you think will happen?"

Liberty opened his mouth to reveal half-masticated food, a brown and red mixture of hamburger, bun, and ketchup. The men at the table recoiled in disgust. Liberty closed his mouth, chewed, and swallowed. He said, "We're all gonna die."

Rich jumped up from his seat and stared at Liberty with alarm etched in his features. I said as soothingly as possible, "Sit down, Rich, and finish your meal. Don't listen to these clowns." I pulled at his arm and he sat down.

Amidst the clinking of utensils and the chatter of neighboring tables, a passing GI was heard to say, "The Greek Third Army is marching on Athens."

Immediately, the whole table sobered while Craig asked, "Did you hear that?"

The airmen looked at one another. Even Liberty paused during his meal. Finally, I said, "That's bulljive. You're getting excited over nothing. How does *he* know what the Greek Third Army is doing, supposing there even is a Greek Third Army? Who was that man anyway? I'm not going to worry about something that hasn't happened yet."

Crofoot laughed and said, "Look at Mr. Cool."

The point was made. Just then Craig noticed Liberty's steel gray eyes scanning the cafeteria behind him. They were like two heat-seeking missiles following the same enticing target. When Craig turned around, he saw Sylvia, a well-built, tightly clad, dependent girl. He faced the table, said, "Hot damn!" and a new, passionate conversation erupted from the already excited group.

I finished my meal and, almost on cue, everyone left, each going his own way. I walked leisurely back to the house.

By force of habit, even though it was the afternoon, I locked all the doors and looked forward to a quiet day of reading and listening to the stereo. It was hot. I thought a nice, soothing bath was what I needed to relax. Pete, who was living off-base with me, was at work and wouldn't be back for hours, so I undressed and, taking only a towel, walked through the large kitchen and into the bathroom. Spigots in Greece were not at one end of the tub as in the United States but hung out boldly from the side. I sat on the edge of the tub, turned on the spigot, and waited for the tub to fill. I put the towel on the towel rack and eased myself into the calming water. It was like being born. It was like taking a deep breath of mountain air.

As I soaked, every pore of my body sang its joy of life. I was so comfortable that I was almost comatose. I heard, close by, "Budda, budda, budda." The deep male voice was speaking too fast for me to make out the syllables, but I knew it was Greek. Again, I heard, "Budda, budda, budda." I wondered where it was coming from. I heard, "Budda, budda, budda." I sat up, straight and alert. It was coming from my kitchen!

My mind started racing with possibilities. It couldn't be Pete because he was at work. It couldn't be a friend since neither Pete nor I ever gave out our keys. I wondered who would have the audacity to break into my house in broad daylight. Certainly not thieves. I thought that I must have been imagining things.

I relaxed and sank into the slowly filling tub. I heard, "Budda, budda, budda." I sat up, headed tilted wonderingly to one side as I listened intently.

"Budda, budda, budda." He was in my kitchen! Who could it be? Then it hit me like a scream. The Greek Third Army! Soldiers were in my kitchen! My heart skipped a beat! My eyes widened! They were here to kill me!

In one mighty bound, I leapt to my feet. My leg knocked against the spigot, making a painful whanging noise that echoed throughout the house. I needed a weapon! I saw none. I needed protection! There was none other than the towel. Desperately, I grabbed it and held it before me, hanging limply below my chin. I knew it wouldn't stop bullets or bayonets, but it was all I had. I yelled, "Who's there?"

I heard that horribly menacing voice, "Budda, budda, budda." They were looking for me! They wanted to kill me!

The bathwater, soon to be tainted with my blood, slopped and sloshed coldly about my ankles. I was naked and helpless. I yelled frantically, "Who's there? Who's there?"

"Budda, budda."

In that instant I saw the truth. I was going to be bayoneted, pinned to the wall like a squealing butterfly. The door would be kicked in, just like in the movies, and I would be pierced by foot-long bayonets. I could already feel the blades cutting through my guts as I writhed in agony. I could see the deadly glimmer in the eyes of the enemy. Their cruel, leering faces would show sadistic joy as I cried out in pain.

As panic set in, I screeched, "Who's there? Who's there?" I was almost out of my mind as I expected death to tear in on me. I literally saw heartless, fiendish Japanese soldiers, except that these were Greeks, tearing my living heart from my poor, dying body.

I heard a soft knock on my bathroom window. The same male voice, now subdued, said, "Guy, Guy, open your window."

I caught my breath. I opened the bathroom window a crack and saw Paul, my Greek landlord. He said, "I'm talking to my mother."

I forced a laugh. I tried to explain, a little embarrassed, "I thought you were in my kitchen. It's the acoustics. The acoustics made it sound like you were in my kitchen."

Paul didn't quite understand what I was trying to say. He looked a little confused at my behavior.

I tried another tack. I had just noticed the colorful, immense bruise forming on my thin, once alabaster, leg. I rubbed it and said, "I hurt my leg, but it's okay."

Paul shook his head in confusion and repeated, "I was talking to my mother."

"Okay," I said quickly. "Say hi to her for me." I closed the window and gritted my teeth. I knew the real cause of my shame. I leaned against the bathroom wall, nearly collapsing to my knees. My pent-up frustration almost made me cry. I mumbled, pathos turning into anger, "Damn you, Crofoot!" and almost fell as I stepped out of the tub.

THE MARINE

Athens fell under a curse. The port of Athens, Piraeus, became a port of call for the United States Navy. Now, an air base designed for 500 airmen and their dependents, was, on a monthly basis, inundated by more than 15,000 sailors. Relations between the Greeks and Americans plummeted as the sailors brought their arrogance and violence with them, which they thought was somehow justified by their wads of cash. Each sailor spent more money on his three-day spree than an average Greek earned in a month.

Vlad Pettenkoffer had a confrontation with a couple of sailors in The Crossroads cafeteria. They would have stabbed him when he was arresting them had Vlad not been quick pulling out his .38 Special as the sailors' blades were reaching for his guts. They instantly dropped their knives. They were arrested, brought to their ship, and subsequently released.

Vlad never had good luck with the Navy, just as Liberty never had good luck with Marines. Whenever he was near a Marine, a confrontation was sure to follow. Marines seemed to instinctively hate him, even to the point of throwing sucker punches at him. Liberty once said to Guy, "I don't understand this hatred, but I think it's due to one of two things. Either they think I'm a coward, which more than one Marine has said to me for reasons known only to them, or they intuit that they don't impress me. Talking tough just doesn't do it for me." Then he added, quietly, "Of course, I might be a coward." Guy looked over at him to see if he was joking. He wasn't.

One evening, Vlad and his wife decided to double date with Richard Victor, who had the night off, and his Greek girlfriend. They decided to dine at a Greek restaurant and then to go to the James Bond movie, *Live and Let Die,* at an off-base theatre. Vlad had ordered souvlaki and French fries, which he particularly loved since they were boiled in olive oil and had a firm crust he loved to bite into. The two couples were surprised at how much they really liked one another. They laughed and joked as the night danced with romance and excitement.

Vlad noticed four American sailors at a nearby table. He tried not to look their way, but each time the people at his own table laughed, the sailors fidgeted as if they were annoyed. The sullen, quiet antagonism was enough to quell Vlad's mood, but the others hadn't seen the storm clouds. Vlad counted the bottles of Bud and Amstel piled up next to the sailors and he grew alarmed.

As he turned to his lovely young wife, he forgot himself for a moment when suddenly, a beer bottle smashed against the side of his head. Immediately, Rich was on his feet, but Vlad, bleeding from a dozen small cuts, grabbed him by the arm and said, "Let's go. Let's all go. It's only a scratch." In fact, Vlad didn't want to fight. He'd seen the damage beer bottles could do to a face and he wanted nothing to do with that, especially with his wife present. Besides, in true Navy fashion, the sailors were probably armed.

Rich jerked his arm away from Vlad and rushed the sailor who threw the bottle. Before he reached him though, another sailor jumped him from behind and held him in a half nelson. A third sailor confronted Vlad when he tried to interfere. The fourth sailor, who wanted no part of this, stood off to one side with the women, who were screaming.

The sailor who held Rich threw out his legs so that Rich's face hit the floor with the additional weight of the sailor behind it. His head bounced solidly, three times, but he didn't pass out. Blood oozed from his forehead and his whole head turned a startling red. Vlad now found himself confronted by two sailors. He fought them as much as he could, but finally covered his face as they freely beat him. Finally, amidst the yells, thuds, and screams, the fourth sailor said, as though making a casual remark, "The Greek at the register is calling the police." Immediately, the sailors stopped fighting and ran for the door where the evening swallowed them.

Rich had two black eyes from his fall. Vlad's face had several small, profusely bleeding lacerations. His whole head was black and blue and swelling into the shape of grotesquely deformed light bulb. His lower lip was puffed out and, later, parts of it would be cut away.

Liberty and Guy arrived minutes later. Liberty was so outraged that he and Guy let the women drive the men back to base while they searched "The Strip" for four white guys, Navy, with recent cuts and bruises. Liberty said, "We're handling this *my* way." He was careful to bump into any sailor in his way and studiously turned away in the hopes one of them would jump him from behind. What disturbed Guy more than anything was that Liberty didn't consider the numbers; he was just as aggressive with a dozen sailors as he was with one. Once, he even offered to take off his badge, go outside, and discuss the "situation" with them. To Liberty's chagrin, no one took the bait. When their searches proved futile, they decided to return to base.

They were no sooner through the main gate when they received a call to go to the bowling alley. Three sailors were throwing beer bottles. There, they were to meet Whittle and Bob Siebold, who was on foot patrol, a new post.

The four of them met outside the bowling alley and were on their way inside when they saw three men standing near the outside tables. Whittle pointed at them and yelled, "You there! FREEEEZE!!!"

One of the drinkers panicked, jumped the four-foot fence behind him, and ran. Whittle yelled, "Get him, Liberty!"

Liberty and Siebold ran after the man while Whittle stayed with the other two drinkers. Guy ran to the car with the idea of heading him off. He reached for the ignition and found that the key had been removed. A crowd was watching and he felt foolish as he left the car and ran after the others. He asked everyone he passed, "Did you see three men run by here? Did three men run by here?" Following the trail of witnesses, he caught up with them behind a warehouse. Liberty was standing off to one side while Siebold, Ken Tyler, and two off-duty cops from another flight were beating the fugitive with their fists and kicking him whenever they could. They forced his arms behind him and handcuffed him. Then, they started to slam him, bodily, against the wall of the warehouse.

When the man stopped resisting, Siebold reached into his back pocket, pulled out his wallet, looked at the green ID, and said, "He's a Marine." Then he added, "Okay, let's take him to Whittle." He turned to the off-duty cops and said, "Thanks, guys." As Bob and Guy were leading the man away, someone tripped him and the Marine fell face first onto the pavement. Siebold and Guy picked him up and they brought him to Whittle.

One of the two other men, identified as Navy by their IDs and who had remained with Whittle, saw the condition of their friend and said, "This is unconscionable. This is needless brutality. I'm going to report this to your superiors. Look at the Mickey Mouse way this is being handled."

Whittle said, unintimidated, "We can bring you in, too, if you'd like."

The two sailors backed away.

The Marine was half dragged, half carried to the police car when he started fighting again. While he was being pushed into the car, his head was "accidentally" jammed up and into its door frame. At this, the Marine scraped his heel down Whittle's shin. The flight chief bellowed, "OOOOOOOOOO!" and pulled up his pant leg to reveal ten inches of raw meat where the skin had been ripped off. Whittle yelled, "That bastard! Let me at him!"

By now the Marine had been thrust into the back seat and was lying on his belly. Whittle took his large, eighteen-inch flashlight and beat the Marine on the head until the flashlight burst into a half-dozen pieces. When he was through, Whittle said, "Liberty, get into the back seat. He's your prisoner."

Siebold and Guy resumed their patrols, the two off-duty cops joined the beer drinkers at the bowling alley, and Liberty sat in the back with the Marine as Whittle drove them up base.

Almost by way of apology, the Marine said, "I was in Vietnam."

Liberty said, "So was my brother. He was stationed at Chu Lai."

"I was a helicopter machine gunner. I killed an old man and a water buffalo. It was all pink. It was a ball of pink mist. We were being fired at and I saw an old man on a water buffalo. I had no one else to shoot at, so I shot the old man and the buffalo. It was ... pink ... all over."

Liberty wondered why the Marine was telling him this, as if he deserved the beating. He wanted to tell him that he wasn't beaten because he ran, but because of each and every insult the Navy ever gave the Greeks and the Air Force. The cops had thought he was Navy. By the time they found out he was a Marine, it was already too late. It was the Navy they were beating.

When they reached the office, Liberty said, "Okay, let's go." He was surprised when the Marine quietly followed him into the cell block. Liberty took off his handcuffs and half-expected a sucker punch, but the Marine stood back as the cell door was closed and locked.

Liberty said, "Take care, Marine."

"You, too."

BUGSY

I never liked Bugsy. That was the nickname we had given Jimmy Kloht because of his cold, glassy eyes. One night I had to pull flight line with him, but because of increased terrorist activity, we were placed in separate pickup trucks on the opposite ends of the ramp. Normally, during a threat, if I was tired, I would lock my doors, lower the car windows an inch, then doze. Never did I leave the windows fully open. To me, it was better to be shot through a window than to wake up with my throat being sliced. Tonight, however, I made a point of staying awake since I didn't trust Bugsy. From where I was parked, I could see the dark blue square of his truck outlined by the white shimmer from the light-all units. As long as that square didn't move, I was safe.

Karl Fiennes was on base patrol. When it was time for Bugsy to be relieved, I saw Fiennes race by at 35 miles an hour through the parked aircraft. I saw the police emergency lights flash on his car as he nearly rammed into Bugsy's truck. I smiled, knowing that his heart must have skipped a beat or two in surprise. Ten minutes passed, which was unusual for a simple post change. Then I saw

Bugsy race away as fast as Fiennes had come in, another unusual event.

When Bugsy was off the flight line, I put my truck into gear and drove to Fiennes. I left my own truck to sit in the passenger's side of the other vehicle. I greeted Karl, using a derogatory, generic nickname for lifers. "Hey, Fly."

He responded, "Hey, Fly." I barely sat down when Fiennes asked me, "Do you want to smoke some dope?"

"Are you kidding? I wouldn't touch that stuff with a ten-foot pole. You know that."

Fiennes laughed. "That's what Bugs said."

Now it was my turn to have a coronary. "You asked *Bugsy* if he wanted to smoke dope?"

"Yeah."

"Why?"

"To see what he would do."

"I'd dump the stuff right now if I were you."

"I don't have any. I was just busting you." Then, as if to change the subject, Karl asked, "Did you ever notice how Bugsy never changes the inflection of his voice? It's as if he doesn't have a soul, as if he's not human."

"He's probably not."

We were there for half an hour and I was about to go back to my post when Fiennes received a call over the radio telling him to go to Base Ops and to call the office on line 411, the secured line. I returned to my truck and post when Tech Sergeant Whittle drove onto the flight line and pulled up next to me. He asked, "Where's your partner?"

"At Base Ops."

"If he's got any pot, tell him to get rid of it. Kloht is ratting on him."

"Okay, thanks for the warning." Whittle had surprised me. I had never expected him to do such a thing. After he drove away, Fiennes returned and joined me in my vehicle. He said, "The call was from Crofoot. He's in the office and Bugs is there reporting me to OSI."

I said, "Whittle was here telling me the same thing. We can expect a visit any time now. I hope you don't have anything."

"I told you. I don't have any." With barely a pause, Fiennes said, "I know what I'm going to do. I saw a dead dog on the side of the road going towards Athens. Let's get it and put it into Bugsy's bed. Are you with me?"

"Sure."

"Are you working tonight?"

"Yeah."

"Good. We'll use your car. My car is too noticeable. We'll wait until you're on main gate, then drive through. You won't see us."

"Who's us?"

"Crofoot is off tonight, too. He'll want to be in on this."

"Okay."

The rest of the night was spent waiting for the bust that never happened. Later, Crofoot told them what had happened in the office. When he was relieved, Bugsy immediately raced to the office and called Senior Master Sergeant Burt, the NCOIC of the security police. He told Burt of Fiennes' offer and the good sergeant said, "It's two in the morning. I'll investigate it when I come in early tomorrow morning."

Kloht said, "But he's got the stuff on him! We can nail him right now!"

"I'm not coming out! I'll investigate it tomorrow."

Then Bugsy made his first mistake. He threatened, "If you don't come out now, I'm going to call Captain Kluckholn. He'll do something."

With a sharp edge in his voice, Burt said, "Go ahead!" and hung up.

Bugsy called Captain Kluckholn, the OIC of the security police. "Hello, sir. This is Airman First Class Kloht."

A sleepy voice responded, "Yes?"

"I have something to report." Kloht then told him the whole story from Fiennes to Burt.

Kluckholn said, "That's good work, airman. I'll look into it tomorrow morning. It's zero two thirty and I've had a rough day. It can wait until tomorrow."

"But, sir," Kloht insisted, "we got to get Fiennes right now before he gets rid of his marijuana."

Kluckholn asked sternly, "How do you know he has it, airman?"

"He asked me if I wanted to smoke it with him."

"That's not good enough. Did you actually see it?"

"No. Not really."

"You either saw it or you didn't see it. Which is it?"

"I didn't see it, sir."

"Then how do you know he wasn't lying?"

"He might be, but he should be searched anyways!"

"Are you trying to tell me my job?"

"No, sir. I'm trying to do my duty, sir."

"You've fulfilled your duty. You reported the incident and now let *me* handle it!"

Kloht now made his second mistake. He threatened, "Sir, if you don't come out right now, I feel it's my duty to contact the Office of Special Investigations."

The captain yelled, "You do that!" and slammed down his phone.

Kloht called OSI who sent a man to the office. After listening to him tell his story from Fiennes to Kluckholn, the OSI man called the base commander, Colonel Fontanarossa who then called Kluckholn who then called Burt. Soon, everyone was in the back office except the base commander. Kloht sat quietly and confidently on a stool surrounded by his superiors, all of them sullen and silent.

Kloht told his story from Fiennes to Fontanarossa. When he finished, smiling like the cat who caught the mouse, Captain Kluckholn asked the room in general, "Should we court-martial him?"

Kloht answered, "You bet we should!"

Kluckholn said, "Not Fiennes, you asshole! I'm asking if they want to court-martial *you* for breaking the chain of command!"

Burt then stood up, his face a brilliant red, and placed his hands on his hips. With bits of saliva flying wildly out of his mouth, he yelled, "You *never, never, never* break the chain of command! You've done nothing but get us out of bed in the middle of the night when we should be sleeping! You've managed to embarrass Captain Kluckhohn and me and any investigation we might have ordered is long gone since Fiennes must have smelled a rat by now and got rid of his stash if he ever had a stash in the first place! How well do you know Sergeant Fiennes? You've been here a month. He's been here a year and I think we know him better than you do! I bet his pals have already tipped him off that we're here. He's been known to lie in the past and here you are, an airman first class, demanding that we arrest someone for what might easily be a lie. Done correctly, we would have put him under surveillance. Now that's gone because of *you*!"

Tears were in Kloht's eyes. It was his turn to turn red and to feel powerless. Kluckholn turned to the others. "Let's talk about this tomorrow. We'll have to decide whether we should fry Kloht or let him off. As for Fiennes, you can be sure that if he had anything, and that's a big if, it's gone by now."

They dispersed and left Kloht to brood alone. The next morning, no one filed a complaint against Kloht and no one met Karl and me at the station when we were relieved. Except for Fiennes, the incident seemed to be forgotten.

As soon as we handed in our weapons, we headed off-base toward Athens. I drove and kept looking at the side of the road trying to find the dog. Eventually, Karl said, "There it is."

I looked and saw a completely flat piece of dark, sun-baked meat with tufts of fur sticking up here and there. I asked, "That's a dog?"

"Yeah."

"How do you know it's a dog?"

"It was a dog a couple of days ago. I don't know what you'd call it now."

"Road-kill. It stinks!"

"It'll make a perfect bedwarming gift for that rat."

I said, "I got a plastic bag in the trunk. We'll put it in there." After I retrieved the bag, I gave it to Fiennes and said, "Go get it, tiger."

Fiennes said, "*I'm* not touching that thing."

"I sure as hell ain't."

Fiennes picked up two large sticks lying on the ground and said, "Let's use these. Maybe we can push it in."

The bag was too unruly to allow us to simply push the dog into it. Its edges curled as if it, too, could smell the dog. Fiennes said, "We'll have to lift it."

I said, "You'll have to lift it."

"Maybe if we both tried to lift it with the sticks, we could get it in."

We balanced the dog between us by using the sticks like the prongs of a huge fork. Once the dog was airborne, I shifted one of the bag's edges beneath it so that when the animal fell, it fell into the bag. When this was done, I tied the mouth of the bag and shoved it into the trunk of my Volkswagen. Even there, the odor of the dog was almost unbearable.

I said, "These hot Greek summers sure ripen things up."

Fiennes agreed joyfully, "They sure do!"

That night I was the first man to pull main gate. As planned, I saw Fiennes and Crofoot pass through the gate in my car. They were gone for fifteen minutes during which time they broke into Bugsy's room by using a plastic ID card to slip the door's lock. They dumped the dog onto his bunk. I saw them drive through the gate again with their fists raised in a power salute.

I was consumed with joy. I danced and sang. Bugsy was an enemy and deserved whatever happened to him. It was then that I made my own mistake. For a month Fiennes and I had been arguing over a jeep named John Valeri. I thought John was "cool" and Fiennes adamantly denied it. I thought John hated Bugs as much as the rest of us, so, when John came to the gate to relieve me, I laughingly told him what Fiennes and Crofoot had done.

Immediately, a concerned hand rose to John's face as he said, "Oh, my God! What do you think he'll do?"

Laughing, I asked, "Who? Bugs?"

"Yeah. What do you think he'll do?"

My laughter stopped in midstream. It had never occurred to me to ask, even remotely, what he might do. John's reaction also told me that I had created a witness for whatever might happen. I answered, "Well, there's several things he might do. First, he might do nothing and that's okay. He might go to the captain or to OSI and that's okay, too. There'd be a little stink, but that would pass." I thought a moment, then added, "He might commit suicide, or he might go on a killing spree."

"Do you think he'd do that?"

"What do *you* think?"

"God, he's so weird that I wouldn't put it past him."

"Neither would I."

Valeri said, "I'm going to remove the dog. Promise me you won't tell Fiennes or Crofoot."

"Okay. I promise."

I watched Valeri race down base. As he later told me, he broke into Bugsy's room using his ID card. He took off his jacket so as not to soil it and threw it onto a chair. Quickly, he wrapped the dog into the sheets of the bed, vomited, carried the dog to a dumpster outside of the barracks and vomited again. Next, he ran to his own room and replaced Bugsy's sheets with his own. Then he locked the door and returned to the main gate where, upon reaching me, a worried hand again rose to his face and he said, "Oh, my God! I left my jacket in Bugsy's room!" Again, he raced down base and for the third time that night, Bugsy's room was broken into. John retrieved his jacket.

Bugs never found out about the dog. Fiennes and Crofoot never found out about Valeri. The only satisfaction anyone got was me. I was happy that John had puked twice while foiling our revenge.

THE SHORT TIMER

Sergeant Guy Burrows sat at the cafeteria table with Craig Crofoot, a small, thin, Cherokee sitting directly opposite him. Craig asked him how it felt to be almost home. Guy recited a formula, "I'm so short that I can't stand in a deep puddle." Crofoot grinned as Guy continued. "To tell you the truth, I'm a little nervous. I don't know what to expect. The lifers tell me that there's a depression going on stateside. Pauline stopped writing months ago. I don't have much to go back to and I'm bummed out about the Vietnam fiasco. There's nothing there for me."

Crofoot said, "Any place in the world is better than here."

"I wouldn't be too sure about that."

"You're not going to re-up, are you?"

"No way. It's just that I don't know what to expect. The last time I was back there, I saw civilians literally spitting on GIs as they unloaded from Vietnam. I've been accepted to college, but I'm not sure I can hack it. What'll I do when I'm faced with a bunch of coeds who have lived under pink skies all their lives with mommy and daddy babysitting them and they call me a war criminal?"

A bevy of young, full-bodied dependent girls burst into The Crossroads, interrupting the flow of conversation. Watching them, mesmerized, Crofoot said, "I wonder if it's the climate that makes them ripen so early. Those girls are only sixteen, but they look like they're twenty." He gave them an appreciative smile. As they passed the airmen, a couple of smiles were returned. All energy and laughter, they sat at a corner table.

Crofoot looked at his watch. "Time to get ready." Then he added with mock sweetness, "I'll miss you."

"Yeah, right." Crofoot left to get ready for work while Guy remained at the table, happy to be left alone with his thoughts. Pete Wallich and Bob Siebold had already returned to the world and, within two weeks, he would be returning to the States himself. Pete had successfully disappeared on the USC Los Angeles campus. Bob was working in a Gristedes Brothers Supermarket in New York City, 2,000 miles away from his native Wyoming. Guy had been accepted to Lycoming College in Williamsport, Pennsylvania, and would major in liberal arts. Liberty had at least another year to go, maybe a year and a half. Guy would miss them, already missed them, even that hate-filled rogue Liberty, who had something very attractive, almost lovable, about him, but God only knew what it was.

As usual, The Crossroads was full of activity. Guy thought of the hours upon hours he had sat there and people-watched. Everything seemed to fit together like a well-written poem. Even the orange Day-Glo plastic chairs surrounding the drab gray tables belonged. He liked the lifestyle found at Athenai Air Base. Nearly everyone drove dented, dust-covered cars. Cut-offs, tee shirts, sunglasses, and sandals were the unofficial dress code. Lusty young women flirted with lusty young men. It was a California beach town sprouting in Greece.

To think of leaving it filled him with a quiet despair. Whenever he saw a familiar face, he wondered if it would be the last time he'd see that person. Every walk became, possibly, a last walk, every meal, a last meal. Once he left, it would be final. If he ever returned, he'd return to strangers.

Kneading his Styrofoam cup, Guy watched a Greek busboy go through his routine. First, he watched the busboy clean a dirty table. The busboy piled a tray with dirty dishes. Then he looked up and scanned his probable route to the kitchen. The Greek's eyes sparkled, and Guy smiled to himself with the foreknowledge of what would happen next. The Greek quickly picked up his tray and filed his way through the packed tables. Like a frog's tongue, his arm snapped out to the side and, in a split second, he had an almost empty glass from an airman who was still eating.

Guy appreciated the artwork of what he had witnessed. Greece was hot and dusty. Americans habitually saved the last few swallows of any drink, not only to wash down their food, but also to soothe their dry throats. It had become a game for the busboys to take that little pleasure from the Americans, who, in turn, tried to prevent them from doing it.

Guy was about to leave when Richard Victor, surrounded by a pack of dependents, joined him at his table. Guy was surprised at how quickly Rich had found his niche. He attributed it to his relative youth. Rich asked, "What happened at the gate last night?"

"Nothing much. A Greek taxi hit another Greek on a motorcycle as they were coming on base from different directions. I heard a loud bang and when I looked up, I thought I saw a taxi with an extremely ornate grill, with someone standing in front of it. It was the motorcycle I saw. As I watched, the motorcycle and its driver kind of peeled off the car in slow motion. I don't think anyone was hurt. There was a lot of screaming and yelling, then they both drove away."

It suddenly occurred to Rich that he should make introductions. He said, "Everybody, this is Guy Burrows. Guy, this is my girl, Lisa, and her friend, Diana. That's Bob. This is Linda and the ugly guy next to her is Gregory."

Greetings were exchanged and to Guy's surprise, Lisa had an accent. He asked her, "You're Greek-American?"

"No," she answered. "I'm Greek. Period."

"You speak very good English. You dress like a dependent, too." Guy paused, trying to pinpoint another characteristic. He said, "You don't have the singsong voice of a Greek woman, but it's musical in its own way."

"Am I being complimented or analyzed?"

"Both, I guess."

Lisa teased with a subtle smile. "You look German."

"I know. Is that a compliment?"

Lisa leaned toward him, a world of meaning behind her laughing eyes. "Of course."

He would have reached for her hands and held them had he not known that Rich was dating her. Solid, heavy seconds passed in which the pair seemed to be the only people on earth, but Guy pulled back and the moment was lost.

The following week saw Guy become a part of a social life which he had only glimpsed in the past. Coffee breaks became group activities. He was never alone.

One afternoon, Rich, who lived in the barracks, asked Guy if he could use his apartment. Sure. He then offered, "If you want, I can fix you up with someone."

"That's not necessary. Tell me when you want the place and it's yours."

Rich said, "Lisa and I are going to the movies this afternoon. Diana is coming along and we thought you'd like to join us."

"Sure, if you want."

"Good. They're waiting outside for us."

Guy chuckled. "Holy cow, that was quick."

"Yeah, well, why waste time?"

The young men joined the young ladies and they went to a movie theatre in Glyfada to see *Enter the Dragon*. Afterward, they walked to a Greek diner to have souvlaki and, Guy's favorite, French fries boiled in olive oil. During this time, the conversation between

Lisa and Rich was desultory with a weak comment added here and there by Guy. Diana didn't say a thing.

As if on cue, the two couples left the diner to wander to Guy's apartment. He brought them into the living room, which had no chairs, but a thick mat of flakati rugs instead. A stereo system sat on two boards supported on either end by cinder blocks. No one that Guy knew owned a television.

The evening was settling in and it was getting dark. Guy lit a handful of candles and put *Tea for the Tillerman* on the stereo. He gave a glass of Coca-Cola with lots of ice to each of his guests. The conversation still hadn't picked up and Guy was wondering what they were waiting for. Lisa asked him, "How much longer have you to stay here?"

"A few more days." Then he recited another formula. "I'm so short that I can't smoke a long cigarette."

"You smoke?"

"No, that's just a saying."

"Are you anxious to go home?"

"I haven't been home in three years. I keep wondering what I have to go back to."

"Beautiful women? Maybe a girlfriend?"

"No. My dog misses me, but he's the only one I'm sure of." At the thought of Jake, his handsome, well-behaved, German shepherd, Guy let slip a smile.

Lisa said, "That's the first time I've seen you smile. You have a nice smile. You should do it more often."

The world skipped a beat. The flickering candles and the dark silence of the night focused on the two of them. Rich and Diana were simply presences in the room. Rich broke the spell by asking, "Do you mind if Lisa and I use your room?"

Guy had expected the question. "No, not at all."

Rich took Lisa's hand, helped her to stand, and led her to the bedroom. When they were gone, Guy was left alone with Diana. He wondered if he was supposed to kiss her. Leaning forward, he asked in English, "Do you like music?"

"Yes." He had hoped for a little vivacity. The curt answer had him stumped. She didn't seem to want to be there. She sat, immobile, like a lump of dirty laundry.

He tried again. "Do you live in Athens?"

"Yes." Guy's eyes widened. He was close to panic. How could he get her to talk a little?

He asked, "Glyfada?"

"Yes." Guy calculated that this would be a very long night if Rich and Lisa stayed in the bedroom for the next hour or two.

"By the beach?"

"Yes."

He rummaged his brain for more questions. He didn't know what was expected of him. In an effort to escape the room, he asked, "Do you want another Coke?"

"No."

"Something to snack on?"

"No."

Guy decided to make one last effort. "Have you ever been to Porto Rafti?"

"No."

Now he waxed poetic. He became animated. A sparkle flashed from his eyes as he said, "I've gone camping there a lot. The stars are so large and bright that half the time I think they're going to fall into my lap." He paused, hoping that Diana would pick up the conversation. However, his hopes were dashed to pieces against her placid demeanor. Sighing deeply, he decided to wait out the duration which, to both his delight and surprise, was amazingly short.

A handful of minutes had passed when they were rejoined by Lisa and Rich. Guy calculated the seconds it must have taken for them to undress, the second or two it took to lie in the bed, and the seconds it took to give a couple of kisses before penetration. They must have taken a couple of seconds to sigh and relax after orgasm. That left about half a second for fornication.

Lisa sat on the rug next to Guy while Rich, followed by Diana, took the empty glasses to the kitchen to be refilled. She said quietly, "It's always like that. Every time I'm with him, we go off somewhere, he gets his pleasure, and that's it until the next day."

She rubbed her hand against the soft rug and said, thoughtfully, "I noticed you have a guitar in your bedroom. Do you play?"

"Not well. I'm my own best audience."

"Do you mind if *I* play?"

"Be my guest."

By the time Lisa returned from the bedroom with the guitar, the Cokes had arrived. Guy turned off the stereo. All four young people sat in a comfortable circle while Lisa sang a Greek folk song, swung into an American folk song, then back into the Greek. She was talented enough to perform on stage. For a wistful moment, Guy saw himself beside her, performing as her backup guitarist and singer. She handed him the guitar. "Now it's your turn."

He said apologetically, "I have to look at the music." He started singing "Stewball," a song about a dancing, prancing, quick-as-the-wind racehorse, a true Dionysian beast, a happy-go-lucky animal that always won his races. For Guy, it was wish fulfillment; he would have loved to be like Stewball.

Next, he sang some airport songs. One was "Leaving on a Jet Plane," where the narrator has his bags packed and is ready to go, just like Guy. Another song was "In the Early Morning Rain," where "this old airport" has the narrator "down" and he'd best be on his way.

Finally, he sang "Hangman," by Peter, Paul & Mary. It was about a man about to be hanged unless someone paid his fee. His father, mother, and brother had not paid his fee and had come to see him hanging "from the gallows tree." In the original song, his lover pays the fee and saves him. In Guy's version, she, also, has come to see him hanging. It looks bad for the narrator until he sees his dog, Jake, come running many a mile. Where the characters of the story talk to the narrator, Guy imitated a dog barking and then translated by singing, "Yes I've brought you hope. Yes, I've paid your fee, for I've not come to see you hanging from the gallows tree."

The last song earned him a laugh from the others. He returned the guitar to Lisa who sang deeper into the night. Between songs she asked him, "Do you have to leave right away?"

"No, but I want to go back."

"Why don't you stay here a few more weeks?"

"I don't know. I got things to do."

If she had asked him what he had to do, he could not have answered her. Lisa was kind enough not to pursue him.

It was almost midnight when she finished her last song. As the others were getting up to leave, she lightly took his hand and whispered, "Please stay."

It was much as Joshua must have felt when first viewing the valley of Jordan. The emptiness he had been living in for the last three years seemed to be intolerable. Here was someone who could fill that void.

Guy saw his three guests to the door. Lisa held back. He whispered, "I'm sorry. I want to go home."

HOME

Newly promoted to buck sergeant, Claudius Boatman made the mistake of going home. Pete Wallich, Guy Burrows, and Bob Siebold had all been discharged from the Air Force, the first two to attend college and the last to join the workforce. Although he found it hard to admit to himself, Liberty was lonely.

The trip began, after his leave request was approved, with Base Ops. He thought he could save money by catching a hop to Germany and then to the United States. He saved the money, but it took him 48 hours, mostly waiting to catch the hop. If he had taken a civilian airliner, he could have made stateside in eight hours. Once on American soil and still in uniform, he took a cab to the nearest civilian airport. As he walked through the terminal, he could see the people staring at him. Here was the enemy, a nation that betrayed its own soldiers.

Hate works. It gives the outsider strength, and Liberty hated these people. His hate gave him the strength to walk through the civilian airport and look people right in the eye. He half-expected to be handed a bagful of dog shit or at least to be spit upon, which would lead to his arrest for violent assault. He might end up in jail, but his antagonist would have no teeth.

But here was the surprise. The people did stare at him. They could see his contempt of them, but they were, for the most part, indifferent. America was pulling out of Vietnam, Congress was finalizing its betrayal of the South Vietnamese, and now it was time to move on, except for the hatred roiling in Liberty's soul.

He found a men's room where he could change out of his uniform and into his civvies. His green duffle bag was still a giveaway but civilians frequently used them, so he gave an inward sigh and relaxed a little as he set about to catch his flight to Rhode Island.

After landing in Warwick, his mother, Martha, picked him up at T. F. Green Airport. He threw his bag into the trunk and got into the passenger's side of the car as his mother drove for home. He asked, "How have things been?"

"Oh, fine."

"How's Alice?" Alice was his sister, his senior by six years. She was schizophrenic. When Claudius was three years old, she was nine. When he was six, she was twelve. When he was ten, she was sixteen. The difference between their ages was significant. Claudius was frequently assaulted by his sister and without warning. It was hard for him to laugh or to show any emotion, since it might unwittingly provoke from her a bellow which was immediately followed by a screaming charge and savagely flailing arms. His stomach would turn and his first instinct was to run away, but he always stayed and fought it out with her. When he was older, in his teens, and physically superior to her, then he'd make a mad dash for the door and run out of the house, not wanting to hit his sister and a woman to boot.

"She's fine."

His mother seemed to be defensive; the tone of her voice was weak and seemed to invite inquiry. "What's wrong?"

"Oh, nothing."

"I know there's something wrong, so level with me. You'll only cause me to worry if I don't know what's wrong."

"Nothing's wrong."

Then it suddenly occurred to him and he asked, "Is Alice beating on you?"

"Well, no. Well, not now."

"What do you mean 'not now'?"

"After you left, she started to attack me, but Max kept her off. Then one day he was out in the yard and your sister came at me. That's when your brother dropped by, saw the bruises, and had her admitted to the Medical Center. She was there for a month and that settled her down a lot. She's on medication."

"I told you years ago she needed medical care. She used to beat on me all the time."

"What?"

"She used to beat on me all the time. You mean you didn't know?"

"This is the first time I'm hearing of it."

"Ask Steven about it. I can't believe you didn't know."

"Your father and I thought we had a nice, peaceful home. You kids never fought in front of us. You must have waited until we were out of the house."

Claudius thought of the many past confrontations with Alice. He couldn't remember his parents at the scene of any of them, but surely they must have known.

"Your sister is seeing a psychiatrist, Dr. Pound."

"I think it was Samuel Butler who wrote that a family is controlled by its sickest member. I guess we know who that is."

"Alice."

"No, Steven." Claudius laughed after giving his brother's name, vowing he would not visit Steven's family while home. Then he added, "I suppose Congress is controlled by its sickest members, too."

When they arrived at the family's ranch house, he was greeted affectionately by his sister. In between their childhood conflicts

109

were moments of great tenderness, feeling, and kindness. On one side of the house was a cherry tree. Claudius remembered how Alice had spent a long evening hanging pieces of candy from its branches with fishing line so that Easter morning her younger brother could wake up to find a candy tree in the yard.

Max was overjoyed to see him. He curled his lips in a ferocious snarl that was his way of smiling. The dog was a true pit bull, loyal to the family, but most loyal to Claudius while hating all other people and other dogs. Max knew that his master's return meant eight-to-ten-hour walks in the woods with no restraints except time.

As Claudius unpacked, everything was quiet in the house, but as evening approached, he could hear his sister talking to herself. There were pauses as if she was receiving an answer from some invisible party to a conversation. At one point, he heard in a strange, tight voice, "I have a rat to kill!" He didn't know who the rat was, but that night, before he went to bed, he hauled his bureau squeaking and scraping across the floor to block his door so that he would not wake up to a hammer smashing down on his skull. This was a precaution he had taken many times before.

Within days he had settled into a routine. Long, long walks with Max through the fields and woods of Whipple's Farm followed by supper with Alice and his mother, which in turn was followed by a walk to Cape Cod Creamery. His mother's house was in the suburbs, but he reached one of the ugly shopping malls then coming in vogue by cutting through the woods. Each evening his mother warned him, "Be careful of that gang on the corner. Be careful." Every evening he'd look for a gang and never saw one. Finally, he asked, "What gang are you talking about? For the life of me I haven't seen any gangs."

"The gang at the end of Patton Road."

It dawned on him who she might be talking about. He asked, "How old are these gang members?"

"About sixteen."

"I'm supposed to worry about sixteen-year-old kids?"

"They might be armed; they might have knives."

"Believe me, they're far more in danger from me than I am from them. I don't think they'll bother me." And they didn't.

Claudius was home for thirty days and those thirty days seemed endless. No one seemed real. Perhaps the consciousness that he'd soon be leaving again kept any intimacy from developing.

One evening, just as it was getting dark, Claudius decided to take Max for a walk. He'd have to walk along the neighborhood streets before he came to the farm where he intended to let Max off the leash. As they casually ambled along the well-trimmed lawns, the dog had to defecate. As the dog hunched on the front lawn of one of the yards, Claudius saw a large man open his front door. The light behind him silhouetted his figure so that Claudius could see him stand belligerently with his legs spread and his hands on his hips. The dog was halfway through his job when Liberty started to pull on the leash. The dog tried to follow while defecating and walked in an odd kind of squat. Then he stopped pulling on the dog. He had witnessed military coups, terrorist attacks, massacres, had been beaten and in turn beaten other men, and here was a man worried about a dog shitting on his lawn. He thought, *if that man comes out of that door, I'm going to kill him. Dog shit is such a petty thing to get upset about that he deserves to die. I'm going to kill him.* Claudius waited for the man to come out to confront him and, yes, he would kill; that man would not survive the night. Whether it was intuition or indifference, the man closed his door and left Max and Claudius alone. They finished their walk.

In the middle of his leave, his mother suggested that they visit his great aunt Virginia, who had developed Alzheimer's disease and, after the death of her husband, ended up in a nursing home. The couple was childless, so Andy took care of her until he died of heart failure. His body was in the bathroom for three days before a neighbor reported to the police that she thought something was wrong at the household. She had seen Virginia, like a shadow, peering out the windows of the house, but she hadn't seen the husband for days. The police forced the door and found the body still on the commode, head resting on an arm that was leaning against the sink.

This was before Claudius enlisted and he remembered how jubilant his brother was when rigor mortis had set in and the EMTs had to angle the body through the door. In another three days, Chris, a nephew, had the body cremated; no one in the family received prior notice.

Claudius asked his mother, "When was the last time you visited Virginia?"

"Since before you left."

"You mean to tell me that Steven hasn't once brought you to visit her in the last couple of years?"

"He's never visited her."

"Why? He was their favorite, their baby, while the rest of us were treated like dog shit."

"It wasn't as bad as that."

"Benign neglect then. Some victory to be avenged on an old lady with Alzheimer's."

"They promised to send him to medical school. I told him not to count on it. How can you give money to someone who spends his college time goofing off, flunking one semester and on the Dean's List the next, then flunking out again? Why throw money at someone who's not serious about his studies? Of course, he also blames Andy for his going to Vietnam."

Liberty remembered how bitter his brother was when Andy said that he didn't have the guts to be a Marine. To prove him wrong, Steven enlisted in the Marines, became an officer, and found himself in Vietnam. Claudius admitted, "Yeah, that's true. He does blame Andy for his going to Vietnam, but let's face it, Steven was an asshole before he went to Vietnam and he was an asshole when he came back."

He didn't add what Steven had said to him when he returned from the war: "I went to Vietnam thinking I was a hero and I came back in disgrace." Instead, he asked, "Where did Chris dump Virginia?"

"Please don't use that word. In a nursing home in Danbury, Pennsylvania. Will you drive me there? I've saved some of the money you sent me. I'll pay for the gas and motel and everything."

"Wow, it's a bit of a way, but I'll take you."

Claudius and his mother drove to Danbury. During the drive, his mother said to him, "I received a letter from the Department of Defense. They said that because your brother served in Vietnam, you won't have to go there. That's why you got Greece."

"Oh, good. Another reason for him to hate me."

It was an eight-hour drive after which they found a motel and had supper at a steakhouse. That night they called Aunt Betty, Claudius' father's sister, and a cousin named Eve. They agreed to meet for lunch and then to visit the nursing home together.

The lunch was pleasant, especially since Claudius was a close friend as well as a relative with both Betty and Eve. After the pleasantries, the food was ordered and Betty launched into the tale of Chris. She said, "Lordy, what a time we've been having here. Chris just took over everything. After Andy died, he put Aunt Virginia in the cheapest nursing home he could find. Never once did he ask me for any advice or help and he never told me anything he was doing. I asked him for some of Virginia's jewelry and he said that it had to go into probate. Everything had to go into probate. We had a huge argument and he finally gave me some costume jewelry."

Eve chimed in, "I got an ironing board." Then she gave her throaty laugh.

Martha said, "They said that they were going to leave something for Claudius, Steve, and my other children."

"I've seen the will; Chris gets it all."

Martha added, sadly, "After all those years of friendship. What happened to the tin box?"

"You know about that?"

"I've seen it."

"Chris got it; he got all the jewelry, bonds, and money it contained. You can bet *that* didn't go into probate."

After the lunch of hamburgers and French fries, they went to Happy Hills Nursing Home. The front of the building was anything but congenial. Its facing was aluminum supports and panes of glass that let in so much sunlight that anyone sitting in the front room felt like they were being slowly cooked. The light was glaring and people had to squint to see. Upon entering, there was a small room immediately to the left that had a couch and a couple of chairs and looked comfortable.

Directly to the front was a large linoleum black and white tiled room. It was large enough to hold most of the nursing home occupants during activity night. In mid-afternoon, its back wall was lined with eight old women, all in wheelchairs, all of whose laps were covered with white blankets, all of whom had white hair and all of whom had pasty, white skin. To the uninitiated, it would have been difficult to tell them apart. They were like living statuary, placidly observing their portion of the world, perhaps judging their past lives, perhaps judging the people visiting the patients like Furies planning their revenge.

The four went up to the front desk where Betty asked for Virginia Durant. They were led down a corridor heavily lined with aging bodies tied to geriatrics chairs. Most seemed to hang in them with no spark of life except, perhaps, to eat one more meal. Drool slobbered from the mouths of most of them and it was the rare patient who looked conscious enough to say hello. Claudius fearfully thought, *one day I'll end up in a place like this, if I don't get killed first. Here's hoping!*

The attendant brought them to Virginia's room. There were no flowers, no books, nothing to remind Virginia that she was once loved and still loved by those visiting her. Claudius sadly wondered, *once she was a child, a little girl, the light in the eyes of loving parents. Where are they all now? What happened to that little girl?*

114

Virginia sat in a geriatric chair, resting her arms on its table top which, effectively, had her trapped. They wheeled her into the small room near the entrance where there was light, in contrast to the dungeon-like, dark bedroom.

Virginia had eyes that sparkled like blue Venetian glass. When she smiled, there was true delight in her wrinkled, mischievous face, a remnant from a better, greater past. Claudius said, "Look how beautiful she is!"

Eve asked, "Virginia, do you know who I am?"

She shook her head no.

Betty asked, "Virginia, do you remember me?"

Again she shook her head no.

Claudius' mother, Martha, asked, "What about me?"

She shook her head no, then she looked at Claudius. When Martha asked, "Do you remember this young man?" she answered, "Sure. That's Claudius." Her face lit up when she added, "My buddy."

Claudius' emotional distress was palpable. He could feel, literally, his heart strings being torn asunder. She looked carefully at him and said, "Here's a man who's not afraid of fire! Let's light this place on fire and get the hell out of here! Claudius, you can do it. Let's you and I get out of here!"

Claudius didn't know how to respond, so he stared at her with tearful eyes. She turned toward his mother and said, "In all my life, I never thought I'd end up in a place like this." Then she pleaded in a little girl's voice, "Please get me out of here."

The others lied to her, telling her that they would get her out of there once she felt better, but she corrected them. "I'll never leave this place alive."

Eve asked, "Virginia, if we took you out, where would you go?"

"Why, with *you*, of course, travelling with you." She paused, then added, "I saw Mom."

Martha repeated, "You saw Mom?" There was only one mom in the Boatman family, a bulldog of a woman whose photos showed strength and determination, a true matriarch and a descendant of a woman who had been scalped during the French and Indian War and survived. Mom had died fifty years ago.

Virginia continued, "Yes, I saw her last night. She told me that they're coming on the train for me. I have to catch the train." The others exchanged knowing looks, but Claudius refused to join in the silent collusion. After all, he believed in signs and spirits and thought that she might very well have had such a visitor. Like the soldiers at the beginning of Hamlet, the only things that Claudius really feared were ghosts. How did Shakespeare intuit this about soldiers? Could he have overheard it in a pub?

Betty said, "The old-time Boatmans used to live near a train station." But Claudius understood what Virginia was saying. The train was a metaphor for death and she was telling them that, soon, she was going to die.

Virginia reached for Claudius' hand and held it with all her feeble strength. Leaning toward him, she confided, making huge circles with her other arm, "Isn't it marvelous how everything goes in a circle. You're born, you die, a complete circle. Isn't it wonderful?"

Virginia soon grew tired and when she realized that Claudius was not there to save her, she sighed and crumpled within herself. If Claudius had the money, he would have torn her out of that place in half a heartbeat, but poverty is stronger than love and he knew he had to leave her behind.

It was a short visit. Claudius had thought to bring her a picture book of horses. He gave it to her and wondered what had happened to her large collection of ceramic horses. What had Chris done with it? She took the book and happily flipped through it like a child with a favorite gift. When the visitors stood to leave, Virginia suddenly reached over and gripped Claudius' hand. She begged in a tiny, pitiful voice, "My buddy. Stay with me. Please stay with me."

Claudius, nearly overwhelmed by sadness, the congestion of grief, answered softly, "I can't." He released himself and quickly left the room.

Claudius had one more visit to make before he returned to Greece; he wanted to visit his childhood friend, Fitz. As a child, Claudius was extremely unpopular with the neighborhood kids. He didn't play team sports, still believed in justice and truth, and refused to be bullied under any circumstances. He also had a value system based on courage, a gift from The Heights, the housing project where he spent the first ten years of his life. When his family moved to the Plat, he found the boys there singularly lacking in courage; they only fought boys a whole head shorter than they were. Thus it was that Claudius was almost always alone.

One spring day, when he was eleven years old, he was walking in a field of the neighboring dairy farm. It had rained heavily and a huge puddle had formed, almost a small pond. Claudius, with his dog Ginger, was wading through the puddle, watching the sloshing water flow around his plastic boots, when he heard someone call to him. He turned and saw a boy his own age, straddling a bicycle, calling to him and waving. At first, he thought of ignoring the boy, distrustful of any generous act, when he decided that he would give as good as he got if trouble should start. When he reached the road, Ginger ran to and made instant friends with another dog, Casey. The boy asked, "Do you want to go fishing?"

From that moment on, he and Jimmy Fitzhugh were fast friends. The following days, months, years in Fitz's company were the happiest days of his life. Fitz gave him the most precious gift of all, unconditional friendship. The two boys and the two dogs roamed the Meantacut woods and fields with abandon. Whole summers followed a daily routine of leaving home at 5:00 am after a scant breakfast, fishing all day, and returning home at 7:00 pm to eat and go to bed. During the winter they watched *Star Trek*, ate lots of ice cream, and wrestled. They played ping-pong and darts in the basement and shot at toy soldiers with BB guns. When Claudius started working as an orderly at the hospital and Fitz had quit school to work in a factory, they still met on weekends to bowl. All that ended when Claudius enlisted and Fitz soon after got married.

Claudius telephoned his longtime friend and asked him if he could drop by for a visit. He found the three-story tenement house where Fitz and his wife lived. As he walked up the stairs, he noticed the smell of dry dust, old clothes, and boiled cabbage so common in these homes. Fitz lived on the second floor. When he knocked, Claudius was greeted by Karen, a woman he had never met before since he was long gone when his buddy had married. She introduced herself and left the two men alone in the living room.

Fitz got up, shook his hand, and said, "Hey, Boats, how have things been?"

"Good, good. How about you? How's life been?"

"Good." Fitz was dressed in a baseball uniform. He added, "I can't stay long. I've got a baseball game in half an hour."

"That's okay."

"Do you want something to drink?"

"No, thanks, I'm all set."

The television was on and Claudius, who glanced at it, didn't recognize any of the actors, so he didn't know what the show was except that it was some kind of drama.

Fitz asked, "How have things been?" He briefly glanced at Claudius, then looked at the television screen.

"Good."

Fitz tore his eyes away from the television to ask, "How's the Air Force?" Then his eyes flicked back to the screen.

"I hate the military, but it's been good to me so far. How's married life?"

Fitz looked away from the screen. "Good. I've put on weight. I was never fat until I ate all that ice cream at your parents' place." His eyes returned to the TV. Claudius looked at the television, wondering what was so much more interesting than a friend he hadn't seen for years.

"How's the factory?"

"Good. I'm a stock boy."

"What's that?"

"I work in the warehouse." Now Fitz was staring at the television. A TV crisis had been reached and a woman was screaming something at a docile man. Claudius looked at the screen and saw nothing that interested him.

Realizing that he was an unwanted interruption, he said, "Look, I've got to go." Fitz looked at him. He continued, "I want to thank you for being my friend."

Fitz said dismissively, "It's nothing. You were my friend, too."

"Yes, but when you came along, I was alone; I had no friends. You did. And I want to thank you for befriending me. The happiest I have ever been is when we were kids together. Thank you."

"It's nothing, Boats, nothing at all."

"Well, I've got to go. See you later."

"Sure, later." Fitz stood up and they shook hands. Then Fitz sat down, looking at the television, while Claudius saw himself to the door.

Claudius was happy to leave Rhode Island and anxious to be out of the United States. He didn't belong there. Reality had different colors for him than that presented by the news media and television. He was very much the foreigner.

Even in New York City, at JFK where he was transferring to take another flight, his separateness was made conspicuous. With only *The Histories of Herodotus* in his pocket, he was staring at a long night. The hard, plastic chairs were uncomfortable and had arms that couldn't be lowered so that no one, in particular bag people, could lie down in them. The restaurants all closed at 8:00 pm and the lavatories were also locked at that time.

A college student of about his own age was sitting near him and kept changing his position in his seat in an effort to find some comfort. Finally, he said, "This sucks." He turned toward Claudius and, wanting some company, said, "My father gave me his Gold Card. Do you want to go to the VIP lounge? It must be somewhere around here."

"Sure," Claudius said, and the two young men began their search in the nearly empty, vast, echoing spaces of the nighttime airport until they found the VIP lounge, and used the magic card for entrance. They got two coffees using Daddy's card and found a comfortable spot to sit. The student said, "This is the life, isn't it, better than what's out there," and he nodded his head toward the door. He asked, "Where are you going?"

"Greece. I'm a GI home on leave."

"That's nice. I go to Brown. I'm on my way to the Bahamas. A buddy and I went there last year during semester break, met two babes, and spent the week riding mopeds around the island with the girls. It was great and we hope to do it again this year. He's supposed to meet me there." The student went on to describe in detail what had happened that year and what he hoped would happen this year. He was young, handsome, and wealthy, and Claudius envied him, but in a good way, without the green-eyed monster part. He wished that he was going on spring break, too, and maybe some day he would, except that he'd never have the money to go to the Bahamas. Claudius listened, the student talked for hours, and it was fun to meet someone whose dreams seemed to be in the act of fulfillment, someone not bitter and disillusioned. Not once did he mention Vietnam or the military and for all intents and purposes, they did not exist for this pleasant blueblood. He never once worried about the draft. They parted with the morning to catch their respective flights. Claudius thanked his one-time friend for his kindness.

It was a harsh, sunshiny day that beat down on the metal surfaces of the taxis, black asphalt, and the metal and glass of the civilian airport. The flight had been long, and Liberty wondered if he should walk to base with his bag to sign in or spend the sixty drachmas for the cab. He chose the cab, found one, and got into it. He said, "Americaniki Vahsis," which told the driver that he knew the route so that he wouldn't take the long way around for the additional fare. He was driven directly through the gate into the police

120

station parking lot where he got out, pulling his duffle bag after him. After he paid the driver, who immediately left, Liberty looked at the gate, waved at the guard, then looked down Main Base Road where he'd have to go to sign in at Personnel.

Staff Sergeant Frick pulled in behind him in the flight chief's station wagon. Still behind the wheel, he asked, "Need a ride?"

"Yeah, to Personnel."

"Hop in."

Leaving his bag at the office, Liberty took shotgun. As Frick pulled out, Liberty took a deep breath and sighed. Frick asked, "That bad, huh?"

"I never thought I'd say this in a thousand years, but it's good to be back."

THE MAILROOM

Liberty sat in the kitchen of the house that he rented with George Finkbinder. He sat on one of the two chairs at the kitchen table. The only other pieces of furniture in the house were the two beds and a stand for George's stereo. Liberty worked nights and had slept late. When he woke up, there was a pool of sweat in the small indentation of his solar plexus and sweat ran down the sides of his body like water squeezed out of a sponge and onto his torso. His sheets were soaked. He was groggy from having overslept and not a little disappointed that he had gone to bed and slept the whole day through to wake up with just enough time to get ready for work again. Although it was six o'clock in the evening, he got out of bed and ate a breakfast of two pounds of cherries and a cup of tea. He would eat his other meals at the cafeteria on base.

Liberty almost never read the papers, but George was a news junkie so there was always a newspaper on the table. While his tea heated on the stove, Liberty looked through the *New York Times*. On the front page he saw a picture of a dozen college students, both men and women, playing leapfrog on a beach in Ft. Lauderdale. The caption said that they were on spring break. They were scantily clad; legs and breasts bounced everywhere in the photo. Liberty sighed. Somehow, it seemed immoral for them to be having such a good time when so many of his own friends were in Vietnam and so many others in places like Greece. It didn't seem right. Yet, he admitted to himself, he would have sold his soul to have been one of them.

After thumbing through the paper, the airman took the tea off the burner. He used his kidney shaped, iron mess kit cup as his tea pot. He threw a tea bag into it and waited for the iron to cool so he could drink without burning his lips. He went into the living room, put Bob Dylan's *Billy the Kid* album on the stereo, and re-turned to the kitchen to watch the flies.

Three kinds of flies occupied the kitchen. There was the reg-ular everyday housefly. Then there was the mountain fly which was a much larger version of the housefly and therefore considered a trophy animal when he and George had their fly killing contests. They were magnificent flies that would swoop through the kitchen's open window and pause defiantly on the edge of the sink, flexing their muscles and looking directly, challengingly, into your eyes. The first time one of these beasts had come into the kitchen, both George and Liberty were stunned by its size and arrogance. Liberty rolled up the sleeves of his shirt, grabbed a rolled-up magazine, and said, "I'm going in." That was the first time anyone had scored on a mountain fly. The third fly was much smaller than the housefly and was, liter-ally, shaped like a jet. These last flies circled endlessly over the kitchen table and frequently engaged in vicious dogfights like com-bat flying aces. For months Liberty held the fly-killing record at twenty-three, but was surpassed when George had a glorious even-ing with thirty-three kills.

While Bob Dylan sang about guns across the river aiming at you, Liberty sipped his tea and spit his cherry pits into an empty bowl. As Bobby was telling him that they didn't want him to be so free, Liberty was donning his green fatigues for that night's duty.

Cutting through the fig orchard at his back door, he walked the two blocks to Athenai Air Base. Finkbinder, who was working main gate, waved him though while commenting that Liberty got uglier every day. Liberty snorted his contempt for such a piddling lie and walked the short distance to the gun room.

The night shift was being issued its weapons and portable radios. It was convenient that it was still daylight, since Athens had a nightly blackout. Because of the impending war between the Greeks and Turks over Cyprus, where fighting had already broken out, the shifts had been lengthened from eight hours to twelve. Manpower was doubled by making two police flights out of the normal four.

Liberty had finished loading his .38 Special at the gun barrel when Ken Tyler's huge weightlifter frame blocked the doorway. Ken paused for a moment of suspense, long enough to let the members of the flight see that he had a Luger stuffed in his holster. His massive right hand moved, whipped out the pistol, and shot at a photograph on the wall. The president was hit above the right eye. He reloaded and scored a second hit on the president's left cheek. The two rubber darts stood out of Nixon's face like two misaligned horns.

Ken held out his gun hand and said, "Looks real, don't it?" The group of men, sitting at odd angles on the chairs and desk, laughed. Even the lifers like Whittle laughed as Ken plucked the darts off the glass surface of the photo. He put the plastic gun into a pocket of his MA-1 jacket.

Whittle said, "I guess you don't like Nixon."

Ken shrugged his shoulders and said, "He's all right. It's Congress I hate." No further comment was necessary since every man there despised Congress.

After the .38 Specials and M-16s were issued, Whittle called guard mount. The flight lined up in a single line before the three-room police station. Whittle called, "Attention!" His eyes scanned the line of green Air Force fatigues, the uniform for recalls. "At ease, men." The flight relaxed. He called into the office to the Greek interpreter, "Yiorgos, get out here! I think you should hear this."

Yiorgos burst from the office and walked down the line of police. Stopping briefly in front of Liberty, he shook his head sadly in mock sorrow, then joined the line at the far end.

Whittle continued. "Listen up. There's been more fighting in Cyprus today. The Greeks are mobilizing their whole male population. You, too, right, Yiorgos?"

"That is correct."

"Athens is still in blackout condition. When you're driving, you can't use your headlights. You can't use any lights at all, including the dome lights." Whittle looked pointedly at Liberty. "That means, Sergeant Boatman, that you won't be able to read on post, which you know is a court-martial offense."

"Gotcha, Sarge. I'm a sharp troop!"

Whittle started in annoyance as a titter ran down the line. It was evident that the flight chief was making an effort to control his anger while smothered laughter kept erupting from the ranks. He said sardonically, "You're a sharp troop all right!"

The flight chief paused to calm himself. He continued. "There's a real good chance that the Turks will bomb the runway and the Greek airbase next door. The Greeks are a courageous people, but their ordinance is no match for the Turk fighters. If there is an airstrike, it's likely that we'll be hit, too. The only thing we can do right now is wait. Are there any questions?"

No one moved.

"Good. Now here are the assignments." He rattled off the posts and corresponding names. Ken Tyler and Liberty were assigned the flight line together.

When guard mount was over, the two men took the pickup truck with the Easy Rider gun rack above the rear window. They lodged their M-16s there and tested the truck's two-way radio with a sound check. The truck would be their portable guard post for the rest of the night.

They drove to the flight line to relieve the two guards already there. They marked the positions of the parked aircraft on the plotting board and called those positions into the office. It was dark by the time they were finished. Ken was driving and found an incon-spicuous corner where they could see both the blue runway lights, which had not been turned off, and the access ramp from the base. He turned off the truck.

Inside the protective, enveloping womb of the pickup's cab, it was nearly pitch black. However, the contrast allowed them to see everything outside the truck fairly well. Liberty looked in the direction of downtown Athens and found it strange that not one light in a city of over a million people could be seen. It was so still and silent that the night seemed to be holding its breath.

He said, "Out of curiosity, I went to the civilian airport after work this morning. It was weird. I saw an old guy crying like a baby as he saw his son off to war. A younger brother and his mother stood nearby watching in a kind of disbelief. It reminded me of when my own brother was shipped out to Vietnam. My father broke down bawling while the rest of us kind of stood there, stunned by the whole thing."

"Did your brother make it back?'

"Yeah. At least a part of him."

"Was he wounded?"

"No, he's all right."

"That's good." Groaning with pleasure, Ken leaned back and stretched. He said, in a rambling, twanging patter, "I'm so tired I could stretch a mile, but then I'd have to walk back." Liberty could almost see the smile on Ken's face.

Ken next flexed his biceps and said, "My arms feel weak. I'll have to work on curls tomorrow."

Liberty looked at the dark shadows of Ken's arms. They looked like telephone poles. He glanced at the thin, white shimmer of his own arms. They seemed so inadequate. Liberty said in his sharp, jagged Rhode Island accent, "How can a man with arms the size of my thighs feel weak?"

Ken smiled at the oblique compliment. A moment of silence passed that was so palpable that it seemed to pulse. Ken asked, "Liberty, how long you been here?"

"I don't know - a year and a half - two years. How about you?"

"A little over two years." Static scratched out of the two-way radio, a message tossed hopelessly into space. Ken added, "I think I'm gonna extend here for another year until my enlistment is up. Greece is good duty compared to other places I've been. Besides, with my younger brother dead, I don't have the heart to go home. It's strange, but I feel that I've lost more than just a brother. Here, I got a photo of him."

Ken leaned to one side to pull out his wallet from a back pocket. He fumbled inside it, trying to see its contents by the nonexistent light from outside the truck. Ken said, "I got it." He handed the photo to Liberty.

Liberty took off his jacket and draped it over his head. He scrunched down in the seat and tried to get as much of his body beneath the dashboard as possible. When he felt that a safe cocoon had been formed, he turned on his flashlight. He saw the picture of a Black man lying in a coffin. It then occurred to him that the only photographs of dead men he had ever seen were of gangsters and outlaws. Another thought disturbed him. So far, the only Blacks Liberty had ever met were tough, young bucks, often filled with hate. Now he was talking family with one of these tough men - family.

He asked, "When'd he die?"

"A month before I got here."

"Vietnam?"

"No – no, diabetes."

Liberty thought how absurd this whole scene was. He, an American, was crouched underneath the dash of a truck with his jacket over his head, looking at the photo of a dead man, while waiting to be bombed by an ally using American munitions to destroy American munitions of another ally in a war that had nothing to do with him. It was so pathetically strange that he fought the urge to laugh. His shoulders convulsed violently as a laugh tried to force its way out of his throat. He managed to change it into a loud cough and pretended to clear his throat. He was afraid of hurting Ken's feelings; yet, Ken must see how ludicrous everything was.

Liberty turned off his flashlight, lifted his jacket, and stared into the dark where he knew Ken's head was. He could see the shadowy outlines of Ken's features and saw that his friend was serious. He re-submerged himself beneath the jacket, turned on his flashlight, and looked again at the photo. He didn't know what to say, so he said, "Your brother was a handsome man."

"He sure was."

"Two years is a long time."

"They say that you get over it and you do, but not really."

"What about your parents?"

"Oh, they'll get by. They always do."

After turning off his light, Liberty came to the surface and returned the photo to his partner. He said, "Be thankful for what you got, Ken. At least you had a brother that you could love."

"Yeah."

There was no moon, so the night was particularly dark. The stars seemed like huge blueberries, so heavy that they were about to fall into the bucket. Liberty had never realized there were so many. He faced the long night ahead with dread. It would be tediously long. Sleep was the only answer. He asked, "Do you mind if I rack out?"

"No, not at all."

"You gonna watch?"

"Sure."

Like reading on post, sleeping was a court-martial offense and was far less excusable. When two guards pulled post together, one guard watched, not for the enemy, but for the flight chief, while the other guard slept. Liberty curled into a fetal position with the back of his head against the back of his seat and his feet resting against the windshield. He closed his eyes. Briefly, he wondered if they would be bombed that night. Casually, he wondered if he would still be alive in the morning. He was almost asleep when Ken said, musingly, "I had a vision today while I was sleeping. Do you want to hear about it?"

"No."

Angered, Ken said, "You don't want to hear about my vision?"

With a frustrated sigh, Liberty asked, "Is this another one of your ridiculous stories like the one where you were skiing so fast that the air friction lit your clothes on fire?"

"Man! You make me feel like a liar! All my stories are true."

"Like the one where you go off a ski jump, catch the edge of a cloud, and hang on until a helicopter comes to rescue you, right?"

"I didn't need to be rescued. Besides, I was speaking figuratively."

"Right. First, you get me depressed and now you want to tell me a story. I'm really not in the mood for any of your bulljive tonight."

"Bulljive? I've had a vision and you call it bulljive?" Liberty noted a slight, unpleasant edge in Tyler's voice. Ken said, as though confiding an immensely personal secret, "I saw my own death."

Liberty swung his feet off the dash and sat up straight. He knew that a vision of one's own death was a serious thing.

Ken continued. "You know the trouble that the Greeks and the Turks have been having over Cyprus? I dreamt they went to war. The Turks, despite the desperate courage of the Greeks, overwhelmed their army and began a march on Athens."

Liberty barely detected a frivolous note in Ken's voice. He said, "That's far enough. I don't want to hear any more lies."

Ken pleaded, "Have I ever lied to you? Really? Have I once lied to you?"

"How about the time you claimed to have dodged the shrapnel from a hand grenade and caught a bullet in your teeth?"

"That wasn't a lie. That was a parable."

"They're not the truth and you can't tell me they are."

129

"Okay," Ken said, "they're not the truth, but they're not lies either."

"All right, we can call them untruths. I don't want to hear any more of your untruths."

"Sometimes, Sergeant Boatman, you learn the truth by listening to untruths."

Liberty mimicked Ken's solemn tone. "Sergeant Tyler, I don't want to hear it."

"Fine, suit yourself."

Liberty started to reshuffle himself into the fetal position when Ken said, as though his partner had expressed avid interest, "They started evacuating the base. They knew the airbase would be a prime target of the Turk attack and they were trying to get all the Americans out before it came. There were a handful of us left.

"Suddenly, on Voula Mountain, we saw a line of Turk soldiers lining its ridge. The line kept getting thicker and thicker until it started overflowing down the side of the mountain. Captain Kluckhohn runs up and says to me, 'Legend,' he says."

"Wait! Who's Legend?"

"I am. From this moment on I'm calling myself The Living Legend. What do you think?"

Liberty shrugged his shoulders and said, doubtfully, "Well, we all have nicknames. If it works, then use it."

"Good. Anyways, the captain runs up to me and says, 'Legend, we need time. Someone's got to stop them or no one will get out alive.'

"I laughed, 'Ha!' I laughed until I saw that there were thousands of Turks coming down on us. I gritted my teeth, turned to Kluckhohn, and said, 'No sweat, Captain. I'll stop them.' He looked at me with tears in his eyes and said, 'God bless you, Legend!' Then he booked."

Liberty asked, "Where was I?"

"Down on the flight line, whipping your chicken; you were so scared." Tyler continued. "Anyways, I got onto the roof of the guard shack at the main gate. Fifty thousand Turks were bearing down on me. I held up my arm and yelled, 'Halt! Who goes there?'

"They stopped, surprised by my boldness. We faced each other eyeball to eyeball. Then I said, 'Draw!' I flashed out my thirty-eight and fanned it. Six Turks went down, dead. But, alas, I too had been hit. I fell down on one knee and reloaded. I fanned my gun a second time and six more fell down, dead. But, again, I was hit and crumpled onto my other knee. I reloaded and fanned my gun a third time, bringing yet another six men to hell with me. This time I knew it was the end. I fell off the roof and onto Main Base Road."

Ken lowered his head in grief. He faced Liberty, touched his arm gently, and with self-pity said, "The fall nearly killed me. They could see that I was dying. My courage had impressed them and they wanted to give me medical aid, but I refused it.

"Slowly, painfully, I started to crawl down Main Base Road. The Turks couldn't figure out what I was doing. They wanted to help me, but I kept pushing them away. Inch by inch, on my hands and knees, I worked my way down base. Every few feet I would stop, look at the sun, and quote Shakespeare. You know, 'Mount, mount, my soul! Thy seat is on high whilst my gross flesh sinks downwards, here to die,' that kind of crap."

"You know Shakespeare?"

"I was in a high school play." Ken took a deep breath, then said, "It was almost evening when I reached the mailroom. A full moon was touching the horizon. Leaning against the door, I used my body weight to push it open. I crashed to the floor and crawled to my mail slot. Again, I painfully stood up and leaned against the wall. I bent my head ever so slightly so I could see into my mail slot. Then I collapsed, dead."

From the tone of Ken's voice, Liberty knew that the story was not finished. He asked, "Well?"

"Well, what?"

Suddenly, Liberty realized what he was supposed to ask. "Did you get any mail?"

"No."

The night seemed to darken. After a moment, Liberty asked, "When was the last time you got a letter?"

"Besides from my mother?"

They smiled. "Yeah, besides from your mother."

Ken answered, "A year maybe. I don't remember."

Liberty nodded his head with understanding. He tightened himself into his fetal position. He said, "Good night. Wake me up if you want me to watch for you. Otherwise, I'll see you in the morning."

"If you and I have a next morning."

With his eyes closed, Liberty felt himself falling. The sensation was sublime. From the edge of sleep, barely conscious, he murmured, "It really doesn't matter, does it?"

CUPCAKE

They called him Cupcake. Hugh Whitaker was a large, burly man with a simple, sweet smile. He was a little slow and this was accentuated by his lips, which hung slightly open, and the way he slurred his words when he talked.

Ironically, this simplicity made him a target of many GIs and particularly of Frick. Cupcake's crime seemed to be that he was alive. Persecution may find excuses, but in fact, it needs none. Staff Sergeant Frick wanted to nail Cupcake because, he said, he wasn't sharp enough to be a cop.

Liberty, on the other hand, liked him. He was refreshing to a man who hated so many people and so many institutions. Liberty identified with him in some odd way which wasn't explained until Whittle said to him, "Liberty, you and Whitaker have a lot in common. You both stand out from the run-of-the-mill GI. He's more stupid than the average man and you're more intelligent. Neither of you fit in and you're both always alone."

"I'm not always alone. I do a lot of things and I go to a lot of parties."

"Yes, but you arrive by yourself and you leave by yourself."

One of the problems with military life is that the personnel change so frequently. You make a friend in a foreign country, have all kinds of adventures with him, rely on him to cover your back in times of danger, and, when his tour of duty is over, he goes stateside and the chances are that you never see him again. He is replaced by yet another friend who in turn disappears or, if it's your turn, you're the one to leave. Liberty had been in Greece for a couple of years and at least half of the flight personnel had changed. Thus it was that he found himself working in Base Ops, doing customs duty during the day, with John Valeri, a short, dark, handsome Italian-American from New York City.

Customs duty consisted of checking the bags of service members catching a hop on an Air Force plane to either Germany or England and, from there, to the U.S. Fortunately, the customs inspectors, John and Liberty, had the freedom to spot check as opposed to checking every bag. They were to look for illegal drugs. As Liberty unzippered a small piece of luggage carried by an officer, he pointed to a young sailor standing in line with the standard issue green duffle bag crammed to near bursting. Liberty pointed to the sailor and said, "You! Go!" With a forceful wave of his arm, he motioned for the sailor to go around the other passengers and into the waiting room for boarding.

He opened the luggage, found a candle, and pretended to look for seams where it might have been carved out to store drugs, then resealed by melting its bottom. He replaced the candle and took a tube of toothpaste and pretended to look at its sealed base, looking for where it might have been tampered with. He checked the lining of the bag for telltale signs of its having been removed and re-sewed together. The officer, a small man with spectacles hanging on his nose, said with a touch of irony, "Thank you for being so careful and astute in your inspection." Liberty said nothing and waved the officer through to the waiting room.

During a lull in the inspections, Liberty said to John, "A couple of months ago I was called to the Greek airbase to check out something the Greeks found in an Air Force colonel's bag. Do you know what it was? A vibrator. The Greeks had never seen one before."

John chuckled. "I guess you could use it to massage your muscles."

"That's what the colonel claimed."

John looked out the Base Ops plate glass windows and asked, "What's Cupcake doing?"

The two men watched Cupcake get out of the flight line pickup truck and march to the runway entrance to the flight line. He carried his M-16 at port rest. As a small Air Force passenger plane, a DC-10, taxied toward the American airbase, he first stood in the middle of the entrance, then squatted down as if for concealment.

Liberty asked, "What's he shouting?"

"Halt?"

"I think so."

They watched as the flight chief's station wagon pulled up next to Cupcake's pickup, and saw Frick in all his wild-eyed, scowling, black fury march quickly up to him. Standing up, Cupcake listened with his head hanging in shame while Frick violently gesticulated and appeared to be ranting and raving at the airman.

As soon as the issue was resolved, the two men got into their respective vehicles and drove off, while a green follow-me truck, its "FOLLOW ME" sign above the truck's cab flashing yellow, replaced them to lead the aircraft to its parking spot.

John lifted his eyebrows and said, "Wow."

Liberty said, "I'll have to talk to the boy."

Liberty did talk to Cupcake, but not about the flight line. It had become apparent to everyone on base that he and Liberty had some kind of bond between them. Leigh, Vlad Pettenkoffer's wife, upon meeting Liberty in The Crossroads where he was imbibing his morning coffee, said to him, "I have to ask you a favor."

Liberty, always suspicious, asked bluntly, almost in a growl, "What?"

"Can you talk to Cupcake? I asked him if he would accompany me to Athens so I could do some shopping. I think he misinterpreted the whole thing. We took the bus to Constitution Square, got off, and then, whenever we came to an intersection, he'd pick me up and carry me across the street. The first time it was funny, but after that I felt that he was a little too friendly. I found the whole thing to be embarrassing, too. You should have seen the looks the Greeks were giving us. Can you talk to him? I can't tell Vlad because he'd throw a shit fit and there's no telling what will happen."

"Sure, I'll talk to him."

When next he and Cupcake were together, Liberty said, "Hugh, Vlad's wife told me that you and she had gone shopping, that you carried her across the intersections. Is that true?"

"Yes."

"That's not cool. She's married and there'll be problems if anything like that happens again."

"I didn't mean anything by it! Honest. I was just being friendly. I thought it was harmless and I was trying to be nice."

"Yeah, I know, but be nice to someone else, okay?"

"Sure, sure, I'm sorry."

"There's no need to be sorry, just don't do it again, okay?"

"Okay."

Cupcake did find someone to be nice to, a stunningly attractive woman who worked at the American Express office on base. No one knew her name or where she lived or where she was from. It was assumed that she was intelligent because of her clerical work in the bank, but since no one had ever really talked to her, she was simply a mystery. It was even more of a mystery when she and Cupcake were married two weeks after they met.

A couple of months after this, the duty of customs inspector fizzled out, since all the passengers were uniformed military people and the inspections seemed to be silly. Liberty was transferred again to the night shift. Whittle was the flight chief and Bugsy was base patrol. That night, Tech Sergeant Whittle was given an unusual order, to kill the wild dogs on base. They had become a nuisance and had bitten two people outside of The Crossroads. Whittle chose Bugsy to help him.

Liberty was on main gate as he watched the two men get issued shotguns and drive away in separate pickup trucks. It wasn't long before one of the pickups circled the main gate and stopped where he was standing. The gate platform was three feet higher than ground level so that Liberty could see directly into the bed of the truck. In it was a large dog lying on its side with its tongue lolling out of its mouth. Its body jiggled loosely with the vibration of the truck and he knew that it was dead. When alive, the dog must have been a handsome animal.

Bugsy was in the cab and leered at Liberty, obviously pleased with his trophy. He exclaimed with relish, "Look what I got!" He then gave Liberty a weak smile like that of Mussolini in his victory photos.

The problem was that Liberty had some pet peeves and one of them was cops who shot dogs. He knew Whittle was out there shooting the animals, but Whittle wouldn't enjoy it like Bugsy obviously did. Siebold once told Liberty that there were guys in Vietnam who killed kids because that showed how tough they were, that they were "hard core." Liberty felt that cops who shot dogs were in the same category. If a cop had ever shot one of his dogs, that man would be dead meat. It was an act of cowardice and here Bugsy was, displaying his prowess. Bugs wasn't able to read Liberty's expression, so he smiled his weak smile and drove away to dispose of the corpse.

Over the course of Liberty's stay in Greece, a number of changes had occurred and none of it for the better. Because of Navy misbehavior and the bungling of American diplomats, the Greeks had gotten progressively anti-American. Within the flights, the in-fighting amongst the GIs had lost all humor, becoming sinister in its effects. The flights had become larger with newer people so that there were now two or three people for every post.

A month after the slaughter of the dogs, Liberty and Crofoot were pulling the flight line during the night shift. Staff Sergeant Frick was the flight chief, replacing Whittle, who was on leave.

When the two men entered the flight line with its rows of lighted C-130 cargo planes, they saw a large beach umbrella, silhouetted against a light-all unit. Near it were the Phantom jets from Germany, stationed in Athens on temporary duty. Liberty asked, "What's that?"

Crofoot answered, "Beats me. Look, they even have chairs." He was referring to the two guards from Germany who had come along with the jets.

Liberty said, "I never heard of such a thing."

The two men pulled up to the guards. Crofoot, who was driving, asked them, "You guys want anything from the snack bar?"

Immediately, the guards swarmed against Crofoot's window demanding, "Why'd it take you so long to get here?"

Crofoot answered, noting their hostility, "We just got on! If you want, we can relieve you and you can go yourselves for something to eat!"

"Man, we're not hungry, but what we want to know is why you didn't get here sooner?"

Crofoot reiterated, "We just got on duty!"

"Don't you bulljive *us*, man. You didn't come here because we're Black, right? You don't want to help the Black man out, right?"

Liberty answered, "Sorry we bothered you!" Then to Crofoot, "Let's go," and they drove to the opposite and darkest end of the flight line. "Those jerks are only hurting themselves. Unless I get a direct order to the contrary, I'm not going near them. They can die of thirst for all I care!"

After a moment, Crofoot added, "The good news is that Frick won't put up with that crap."

They watched as Cupcake's truck lights pulled onto the ramp and drove to another dark corner of the flight line, away from both them and the guards from Germany. He was also pulling flight line duty. Liberty turned on the dome light and pulled a book from his pocket while Crofoot turned on his radio, both forbidden objects on guard duty. They settled in for the night, at least until post change.

Unexpectedly, a FOLLOW-ME truck driver stopped next to them, got out of his vehicle and asked, "How you boys doing?"

This was an unusual visit and both men answered, a little perplexed, "Fine. Okay."

The truck driver asked, "Were either of you insulted?"

Again, the perplexed looks. "No."

"I said the exact same thing to those guys." He motioned with his head toward the Phantom guards. He continued, "Do you know what they said? They said that they were going to turn me in as a racist because I called them 'boys.' Heck, that's the way I always talk! I use the term 'boys' all the time but I don't mean anything by it! They said they're going to file a complaint and I might lose my career over it, just because I used the word 'boys'!" He paused, then said, totally discouraged, "I don't know. What the hell is this world coming to?" He walked away in disgust, got violently into his truck, and drove to the maintenance hangar.

Crofoot said, "Looks like he's screwed."

"I hope not, but you know how these things work."

As the hours passed, they became aware that something was wrong. No post changes were being called. Although they felt stranded, it gave them more of a chance to read, relax, and maybe catch a nap with one man staying awake while the other slept. Cupcake's pickup hadn't moved an inch. Liberty said, "There must have been an accident off-base," and Crofoot agreed with him.

Soon, they saw a sedan moving slowly towards Cupcake's pickup. Liberty turned off the dome light of their vehicle and asked, "Why doesn't he have his lights on? Who is it?"

"Must be Bugsy." Crofoot keyed the radio's mike on and off three times to make three clicking sounds, an unofficial code to tell the other driver, in this case Cupcake, that someone was on the flight line and heading his way. Crofoot said, "If he's asleep, I hope that wakes him up." The sedan paused at the pickup, then raced away to be replaced minutes later by the flight chief's station wagon. Now, both the pickup and the station wagon left the flight line, leaving Liberty and Crofoot wondering what was happening.

The sedan returned, this time with its lights on, and came their way. It was Bugsy with a strange, pleased, self-assured smile on his lips. He got out of the sedan to stand next to Crofoot's window. Barely hiding his glee, he asked, "Guess what?"

Inquisitive silence answered him, so he continued, "We caught Cupcake sleeping. Frick gave him flight line duty so he'd fall asleep. I kept checking on him until I found him asleep, then I called Frick over the Base Ops secure line. Frick is writing him up now even as we speak. Pretty good, huh?"

Liberty repeated, his voice sharp, clear, and fiercely hard, "Pretty good?" The truck's dome light was off, so that Liberty saw only a dark shadow that was Bugsy and Bugsy, likewise, saw Liberty as a dark shadow.

Bugs said defensively, "Yeah, what's wrong with that? The dope got caught sleeping."

"What's wrong with that? You ruined a man's life, that's what's wrong with it! He got married a month ago and now what's he going to do? What's his wife going to think? What's *she* going to do?"

"That's none of my business."

Liberty's fist shot out convulsively and would have hit Bugsy had he been within range. Liberty's voice became quietly threatening. "I suppose you'd turn me in, too, right? I suppose if you'd caught me sleeping you'd turn me in, too."

"That's right."

Crofoot, who was between them, leaned back in his seat as far as he could go and said, "Wait! Wait! Don't do anything. Let me get out of the way. I'm opening my door now. Nobody move! I'll be out of the way in a minute." He slithered out from between them. He left the door open so that Liberty would have a clear shot at Bugs. Each of the antagonists had a clear view of the other's shadow.

Liberty shifted in his seat so that he was directly facing Bugsy. His right arm was free and he felt the weight of his .38 Special sitting on his hip. Bugsy backed up and said, softly, "I might turn you in." Then he added, loudly and in anger, "What are you going to do about it?"

Liberty leaned forward slightly and whispered, like a lover, "Whatever you want to do about it."

Crofoot was standing at the back of the pickup truck, waiting. A deadly second passed, then a second moment, then a third. Without another word, Bugsy turned away, rushed to his car, jumped in, jammed the car into gear, and raced away.

Crofoot rejoined Liberty. "I could swear Bugs was crying. Well, that was fun!"

Liberty scowled. "Yeah, can't you see me laughing? If that fuck …" then he caught himself. If Bugsy gave him cause, he would kill him, but it was better not to say it, not even to Crofoot.

A year later, long after Cupcake was court-martialed and discharged from the military, John Valeri and Liberty were on base patrol. They were in the sedan and were returning from an incident at the Jet Lounge where one sailor had been badly slashed with a broken beer bottle by another sailor. John was driving and had taken a shortcut, Airport Road. As he was about to pull onto the highway fronting the main gate, a small, white Comet careened out of the sparsely lit highway and slammed into the side of their vehicle. John called Control to inform them of the accident and was told to wait for Tech Sergeant Roger Guiscard, a new flight chief who'd been in Greece for less than a month. From the other car emerged Frick, drunk and bleeding profusely from small glass cuts in his forehead.

Within minutes Guiscard was there. After getting a verbal report from John about the accident, the flight chief said, "Frick's as drunk as a loon. We got a call earlier today from the NCO Club. Frick was thrown out for fighting."

Although the Black staff sergeant had maintained his distance, it was obvious that he was frightened. He kept walking back and forth nervously. Suddenly he rushed up to them and said, "When you guys write up the report, you could say that I ran into you to avoid a serious accident with a Greek on the highway, that the Greek forced me into you, that the Greek driver never stopped but just kept going." Suddenly, having made his plea, embarrassed, he backed away and returned to his Comet.

Guiscard said, "I've been here only a short time. I don't know Frick. I've never worked with him, so I'm leaving it up to you two if you want to fry him or not."

John said, "I've got no gripes against him."

Guiscard faced Liberty. "It's up to you, Boatman. He's drunk, he's been in a fight, and he's been in a car accident. If you want, you can ruin him right now."

Liberty remembered Cupcake and his first instinct was to fry Frick, yet the airman had never done anything to him personally. He saw Frick as another Cupcake, another man who stood out, but because of his strength and hatred. Liberty said, "Let him go. We'll say that a Greek ran him off the road and into us, that if he'd stayed on the highway, someone would have been killed."

Guiscard nodded his agreement that he would put it into the accident report. He said, "Good enough" and walked back to Frick.

As the two patrolmen stood by their car, looking down the empty, midnight highway, Liberty said, "Today is Frick's lucky day. Think about it. Of all the people on base, of all the people who hate Frick, he falls into the hands of the only three people who have nothing to avenge. What are the odds of that?"

THE SAILOR

When Claudius Boatman first arrived in Greece, it was like what he imagined living in Southern California must be like. The 500 Air Force personnel and the 1,500 dependents of Athenai Air Base lived a casual lifestyle of beat-up cars, tee shirts, cut-offs, and sandals. Despite the occasional terrorist attack, it was still better being a security guard in Greece than being stationed in the frigid cold of Minot, North Dakota, or in the killing fields of Vietnam. You did your daily eight-hour shift and the rest of the time was yours.

This idyll lasted about a year and a half into Liberty's three-year tour when Piraeus, just outside of Athens, was made into a port of call for the U.S. Navy. Like Viking barbarians, the American sailors invaded the land. A base designed to service 500 airmen now had an additional 15,000 plus sailors to accommodate. Whereas airmen traveled in groups of two or three, sailors traveled in groups of at least half a dozen, all dressed like the male models in *Playboy Magazine* and many of them carrying some kind of a knife or a razor. If an incident was domestic, it was Air Force. If it was a rape, a bar fight, or a brutal assault, it was Navy. If the Navy couldn't find

Air Force people to beat on, then they found sailors from other ships to beat on and if that failed, they beat on the Greeks. If a fifteen-year-old Air Force dependent ran away from home, she'd be found shacked up with sailors. Liberty hated them.

One night, after the fleet had come in, Liberty was pulling base patrol with Craig Crofoot. Liberty loved the night shift. He loved wallowing in the silence, stillness, and calm when other men were dreaming and the dark hung as though caught on the branches of the trees. In an effort to help explain himself to the other cops, Boatman sometimes said, "The dark can be your friend. The problem with Americans is that they're afraid of the dark. Not me, I love it." Then he'd shrug his shoulders in response to the blank stares that always answered him.

As their car lights cut through the night, Crofoot talked breathlessly about a Hispanic girl he had seen in a park off Ventura Highway a year ago while on leave. As he drove he said, "She had long, bushy hair that waved like a waterfall. She wore a tight, red skirt that was almost above her hips and she had the long, graceful legs of a racehorse. When I saw her, Liberty, I knew, I knew I was in love."

Crofoot knew that Boatman was listening intently, with an appreciative silence, despite the fact that his face showed no expression. Perhaps it was a mood or the subtle lifting of facial lines that let Crofoot know that Liberty was immensely interested. He continued, "You'd love California, Liberty. We have long, rolling beaches, sharp, dramatic cliffs, and the women to match."

Boatman waited expectantly. When the wait became uncomfortable, he asked, "What happened?"

Crofoot asked in turn, "What do you mean?"

"With the Hispanic girl."

"Her? Nothing."

"What do you mean nothing?"

"I was too shy to talk to her."

"That's it? You got me all hot and bothered about a girl you never even talked to?"

Craig defended himself. "But I'll remember that moment forever."

Before Liberty could respond, Finkbinder, the desk sergeant, called over the radio, "Control to Car Four."

Crofoot keyed the mike. "Four by."

"Go to the Jet Lounge and help the Greek police. There's a Navy guy giving them trouble. Pick up Yiorgos on your way out."

Crofoot answered, "Ten four." He returned the mike to its receiver, then asked, "What's the Jet Lounge?"

Claudius answered, "It's a bar on The Strip."

They stopped briefly at the police station to pick up their interpreter. The three men arrived at the bar and saw a huddle of Greek policemen before a small park a hundred feet away. Instead of stopping at the bar, Crofoot drove directly to the policemen.

Boatman got out of the car and paused. He turned his head to one side as if listening. It was so cool and quiet that the calm was almost tangible. Nowhere else in the world had the darkness, the night, seemed so palpable to him. He asked Craig, who was now standing next to him, "Feel it?"

"Feel what?"

Boatman sought for the right words, then said, "It's like being in the mind of God. Feel it?"

Crofoot's face lightened. "Yeah, I *do* feel it."

Yiorgos, who had been talking with the Greek police, returned. He said, "There's an American sailor in the bushes. He's got a gun. They're afraid because they think all Americans are killers. They want one of you to go in there after him."

Crofoot's already energetic frame became even more animated. He made a barely perceptible hop and said, "Hot damn! A gunfight! Liberty, you'll go down in history!"

Boatman dramatically unsnapped his holster strap. Carefully, he loosened his .38 Special. He took long, forceful strides to the path down which the fugitive had fled. It was lined with thick, sinister-looking bushes and trees. Death was somewhere amongst them! Fear was in the air. It was so strong that Liberty could almost taste it. Anything could happen. Anything.

Liberty knew that this was his moment. Keeping his right hand hovering over his pistol, he marched, step by step, into the unknown. He could feel the Greeks huddling behind this mad American who wanted to taste blood. Behind the Greeks followed the more cautious Crofoot.

There was a full moon out so that the path looked like a silver ribbon on black velvet. Boatman expected noise, a sudden rush, staccato shots, gun flashes, and agonized screams from wounded men. He marched ten, twenty, thirty yards and still nothing happened.

Finally, he saw him, a dark lump lying on his belly in a small clearing that might have served as an unholy temple. Without hesitation, Liberty rushed him and straddled his body. While one hand pushed forcefully on the sailor's back, the other searched beneath him for the gun. Liberty felt something warm and sticky. He thought, *blood.*

He found no weapon. He retrieved his hand and held it up in the moonlight. Instead of blood, he saw a thick, pink, liquid fuzz. Bits of half digested, yellowish meat and crushed peas hung from his fingers like rocks on a moonscape. It smelled like sickly sweet vinegar.

Horrified, Liberty yelled, "Puke!" while the contents of his own stomach rebelliously rose into his throat. He swallowed a couple of times to keep it down, feeling a cool, unpleasant thrill at the base of his mouth. In a disgusted panic, he searched desperately for something to scrape his hand. He found a dirty, gray newspaper covered with black grit. He scrubbed his hand until it burned, and the newspaper was a tattered remnant.

It was the final outrage. Silently, like a cobra about to strike, Liberty made a decision. He turned toward his partner but had to wait impatiently until Crofoot could control his laughter. Craig gasped, "I'm almost peeing my pants! You should have seen your face! You looked as though something was eating your hand away!" Crofoot grabbed his stomach, curled himself nearly in half, and laughed out of control. When he calmed down a bit, he said, "I got to find a john. I've got to pee bad."

Boatman said in a bland, toneless voice, "You can piss on-base. Let's go."

He started to walk away, but Crofoot gripped his shoulder. He asked, "What about the sailor? Shouldn't we take him with us?"

"I suppose we should, but we're not."

"If we leave him here, the Greeks will beat him up."

Liberty answered, "That's the idea." He walked away followed by Yiotgos and Craig.

LAST DUTY NIGHT
1974

Liberty had been in Greece for three years and was due to return stateside to be discharged. This was sad in many ways. He had adapted to this strange lifestyle. During meals he now dipped his bread into olive oil whereas, when he first arrived, he thought that it was disgusting to do so. He now preferred the strong, fresh meat from the butcher shops, meat he had initially disliked, instead of the prepackaged, processed pink stuff at the commissary. Like the Greeks, he had developed the habit of staring at attractive Greek women to the point of rudeness. He wore sunglasses, cut-offs, sandals, and always a tee-shirt, particularly on the beach to keep his back from flowering into blood blisters under the hot Hellenic sun.

On base he was highly respected as a man who never backed down from a fight, regardless of the odds. He had earned a black belt in Tang Soo Do, Moo Do Kwan, and was part of a five-man team that took the Greek national championships. Staff Sergeant Frick had come to trust him enough so that, when he opened a bar in Athens, Liberty sometimes used his ration card to buy him liquor for his business. On occasion, he bought audio equipment for Tech Sergeant Whittle who either gave it to friends and relatives of his Greek wife, which was illegal, or sold it in the black market, which was also illegal. Either way, Whittle had been assigned as Chief of Investigations so that he could pull the receipts of the purchases and destroy them, leaving no paper trail. Yiorgos had been promoted to the Customs Office and had also offered, unknown to Whittle, to destroy any of Liberty's purchase documents. Liberty never took money for any of his purchases. In an odd way, Whittle and Frick had become people he trusted and respected, although not quite his friends, and if they asked him a favor, he would do it.

Just as Liberty had started to unconsciously call Greece his home, he received his orders to ship out. Rumor had it, incorrectly, that the United States was in a recession and that there were bread lines everywhere. Having no way of judging the truth of this rumor, he was worried. He had neither girlfriend nor much of a family to return to. His mother had doggedly written to him for all three years, but the rest of the universe was shadow and hearsay. His real world was Athenai Airbase.

Unfortunately, he had been so bitter and hateful, especially towards the Air Force, and had expressed this hatred so frequently and strongly, that to re-enlist seemed like a betrayal of his own stance. Yet, he wished someone, a lifer who he respected, would take him in hand and talk him into staying. No one did. Everyone knew his attitudes, and no one saw the doubt and anxiety behind his stern, hostile facade. Whittle even suggested that he should go to Rhodesia to work as a mercenary since he seemed to have an aptitude for violence, and it was a good way to make money.

Liberty's last official duty night was a quiet, mild night of silent beauty. He felt empty, as though he'd been gutted, to think that he might never again watch the passing of the full moon over Voula Mountain. He had always wanted to go to Mykonos to gawk at the nude bathers, mostly Scandinavian girls. He would have liked to be forced to lie on his belly, like Siebold did, to hide an erection as he watched the women disrobe. But it was too late to take that trip now. He had two weeks in-country before he left and most of that time would be spent out-processing.

The next morning, shortly before he was due to out-process, Liberty was sitting in The Crossroads with Craig Crofoot drinking, perhaps, his three thousandth coffee there. His friend asked, "How does it feel to be so short?"

He answered with one of the formulas, "I'm so short that down looks up." Crofoot grinned as Liberty continued, "I've been accepted by Rhode Island College, but I have no idea what that'll be like. I haven't a family to speak of and I'm pretty bitter about this whole Vietnam fiasco. There's really nothing there for me to go back to. The last time I was there, the civilians were rude and abusive. What if I go to college and some teeny bop calls me a baby killer? What am I supposed to do?"

"You've got a black belt. Beat the fuck out of them! Make sure they never say it again."

"I don't think it's as simple as that."

Both airmen started ogling the young dependent girls with their full, mature bodies that matched the hot, torrid climate so well. Liberty wondered when all these familiar faces would be seen for the last time, never to be seen again – forever.

Sergeant Whittle entered the cafeteria, got a coffee, and, un-characteristically, joined them at their table. He nodded his head in greeting. "Hey, Crofoot. Boatman."

Craig nodded hello and Liberty said, simply, "Hey, Sarge."

Whittle said, "Boatman, I've come to ask a favor of you. I'm flight chief tonight and the Greeks are rioting in town. Ever since the U.S. refused to mediate between them and the Turks, they've been acting up and it looks like it's going to come to a head tonight. We're a little short and we can use all the help we can get."

Liberty cut him off. "Don't bother asking me, Sarge. The answer is no."

"I don't think anything serious is going to happen, but I'd like you there just in case."

"Last night was my last duty night."

"I could pull rank."

"You could."

"Do it as a personal favor to me."

Liberty drank the last few sips of his coffee and started tearing at his Styrofoam cup. He asked, "Did the captain send you?"

"No. It was my own idea."

Liberty heaved a sigh. "All right. I don't want to, but all right."

"Thanks, Liberty." Whittle left, taking his coffee with him.

Crofoot said, "I wouldn't have done it."

"I know. Are you working tonight?"

"Yeah."

"I know you think I'm acting like a lifer, but I wouldn't have done it for anyone else except Whittle."

"I suppose."

That night, even before guard mount, excitement was running high. As the SPs milled about the gun room and office area, a Hispanic airman, who Liberty knew by face only, came curving and squealing in a cloud of dust while driving his maroon Ford Galaxie into the parking lot. A Greek girl sat demurely in the passenger's seat of the convertible while her boyfriend ran into the office to complain and file a report, moral outrage and hurt accenting his voice.

He stood with outstretched arms, all muscle and strength, retelling the event which, judging by his cuts and bruises, must have taken place only moments before. He cried, outrage putting a hurt, unbelieving edge to his voice. "I just stopped at a red light and as I was sitting there, minding my own business, a Greek taxi driver who was behind me got out of his car, ran up to me, and punched me in the face. When I got out of my cab, he started yelling, 'Help! Help! He's an American! Americans are killers!' The first thing I knew, I had fifty Greeks ganging up on me and holding me against my car and beating me. I started yelling for the Greek police and then I saw that a Greek policeman was helping to hold me against the car!" Liberty and Crofoot turned away so that they wouldn't be seen laughing.

Whittle, coming in from the outside, said, "You had better file a complaint and then we'll take you to the dispensary. Is your girl okay?"

"Yeah, they didn't touch her."

Whittle took him into the inside office so that the desk sergeant could begin the report. The cops bantered lightheartedly about the incident. When the flight chief rejoined his men, he called guard mount. Despite the fact that the number of on-duty policemen had been doubled by the off-duty cops, they still numbered only fifteen men to man the posts, many of them new to Greece and very few of them with practical experience.

Whittle said, "You gents probably know this already, but the Greeks are rioting in town. As you've seen, they're beating up Americans in the streets. The airbase in Crete was overrun earlier today and a building burned to the ground. Word is that one cop was killed but that hasn't been confirmed." Looking up from his notes, Whittle said, "I don't think we have anything to worry about. The Cretans are a different breed of Greek than the Athenians. You all know what to do." He then gave out the assignments and dismissed them.

Liberty's partner was Dave Stikker, a jeep. He was a tall, gangling, blond youth who looked a lot like Liberty imagined he had looked three years ago. On the way to the flight line, they stopped at the Base Ops snack bar for the coffees that they would nurse for the rest of the night. They relieved the off-going guards and found a cozy, dark corner on the flight line where, hopefully, they could see and not be seen.

Liberty asked, "Have you ever seen such a beautiful night? After you're here a while, you'll begin to sense a presence here. I don't know if the tourists pick up on it or not. I was here about six months before I noticed it, as if the air itself was some kind of spirit pervading everything. I really don't know how to describe it, but you'll feel it too after a while. It's no coincidence that civilization was focused so long in Greece. It makes me wonder what Egypt and Iraq must be like."

After turning on the dome light, Liberty picked up his book and started to read.

Dave asked, "What are you reading?"

"The Koran. It's on my reading list of the hundred of the world's greatest books."

Liberty read for a little under fifteen minutes when Dave querulously asked, "What do you think they'll do?"

"Who?"

"The Greeks."

"Oh, I don't know. Probably nothing. Why?"

"Do you think they'll get as far as the flight line?"

Liberty saw the chance of a lifetime. He remembered reading, when twelve years old, the Sergeant Rock comics that always had a band of about five tough army guys who consistently foiled the German army. He remembered the frequent scenes of Sergeant Rock running through a gauntlet of bullets that pitter-pattered about his feet and legs, kicking up tidbits of dirt, but never, ever, touching The Sarge. Now was his chance to be The Sarge, The Rock.

He pointedly placed the Koran between them. He sighed and stretched, flexed his biceps, and emitted an exaggerated yawn as he forcefully gripped the steering wheel. Grimly, he said, "Look. You and I are sitting pretty. For any rioters to get here they first have to get through the Greek police, then the Greek army. After that, they have to get through our own main gate and go down Main Base Road for a mile to reach the flight line. Besides, this is a Class A security area. We can shoot anybody we want once they cross those yellow lines. We both have M-16s and .38s and enough ammo to keep any mob off our backs. If worse comes to worst, you and I will get out alive. I don't care if all the aircraft in the Air Force get blown up; you and I will get out of this alive." Pleased with his performance, Liberty leaned back and put both hands behind his head. He said, "You might as well relax and enjoy the night."

Barely a second passed when a call came over the radio. "Control to Car Three." It was Whittle's voice.

Liberty keyed the mike. "Three by."

"Be advised that Airman Wycherly is to relieve Sergeant Boatman on the flight line. Sergeant Boatman is to go to the main gate."

If any place would get hot that night, it would be at the main gate. Liberty visualized himself surrounded by a hostile Greek mob. He answered Whittle, "Ten four," and swore under his breath. Then he said to Dave, "I guess I'll see you in the morning."

At that moment, eight thousand miles away, Liberty's sister woke up screaming. She had dreamt that he had been killed by a mob. Oddly, his mother, who responded to the scream, had dreamt the same thing.

Wycherly, another new man, arrived minutes later after having been relieved from the main gate. He was a small, scrawny man and he was outraged. He huffed his way from the patrol car and nearly hit Liberty in the face with the portable radio as he was getting out of the truck. In a hurt, angry voice, Wycherly whined, "I don't see why I had to leave the main gate! I'm as tough as you are! I mean, I have my green belt in karate and I've studied nunchuks! *That* should mean something!"

Liberty responded, after getting out of the truck and facing Wycherly, "Call in. Tell them that you want to pull main gate. I don't care. I'd rather stay here. I've got nothing to prove."

Wycherly hesitated, then said, "Naw," then got into the waiting pickup, slamming its door with all the violence of his pent-up anger. After taking a long, hard look at the airman, Liberty decided that he didn't like him. He then drove to the gate.

Once there, he was surprised to see no activity at all. Two cops were manning the gate, standing casually, hanging out, beneath its brilliantly white lights, so Whittle called Liberty over to him and pointed to a stack of tent posts. Handing Liberty an ax, he told him to cut the posts into thirds to be used as clubs should the base be overrun. While Liberty did this, another new man, a dog handler named Kevin Braugh, was sent throughout the base to collect ash can covers to be used as shields. When they had collected and created enough clubs and covers, they were informed by Whittle that the Greek police had managed to control the riot and all immediate danger had passed. They then carried their collection of clubs and shields to the gun room for storage for possible future use.

However, another aggravation developed. A band of seven Greeks were beating solitary Americans on Airport Road. They would wait for a car with the distinctive yellow license plates to come down the road. If only one person was in it, they would step in front of the car, causing the American to stop. When this happened, as it always did, they would pull the driver out of the car and severely beat him.

Repeated calls to the Greek police had produced no results. Whittle had a solution. He had Liberty, Kevin, and another new man, Dan Sheridan, strip off their weapons and badges. Then, he had them slouch down and hide in the sedan as he drove it down Airport Road. Liberty found it odd that all four men were of Anglo-Saxon descent and wondered if it meant anything. Four Americans, they felt, were an easy match for seven Greeks, especially with surprise on their side.

Unfortunately, as Whittle drove down the road, he said, "The gig's up. There's a Greek police car. They probably scared the gang away." Despite this, he drove up and down the road twice, but no attack developed.

When they returned to base with about four more hours before dawn, Liberty was given base patrol with Kevin. The two men decided to check doors and hopefully find one open. They found a paint locker open, but since neither of them found anything they wanted, they called it in. Next, they found the legal office open where Liberty took two combination pad locks and Kevin took a handful of pens. They didn't call that one in.

In their wanderings they came across a construction site. Greek laborers had built the shell of a new building. Liberty asked, "Did you ever see those old guys wearing suits and ties coming onto base in the morning?"

"Yeah."

"Do you know who they are? They're the guys who work on *this* place. They're construction workers who come in wearing their suits, change into their work clothes on site, work all day, then change back into their suits again when they leave. They call that dignity."

With the exception of the barracks, the buildings on base did not have lavatories. They were serviced by outhouses with modern plumbing. While Kevin walked to the nearest outhouse, the women's, Liberty roamed about the construction site, checking the doors to the new building. None were open so he leaned against a window and used his flashlight to try to see inside. He saw a hand sticking up in the window and screamed as he fell backward, stumbling flat onto his back. Immediately, he was on his feet and, just as instantaneously, he knew what had happened. It was his own hand reflected from the window. He laughed at himself and joined Kevin in the lady's room. He asked, "Didn't you hear me scream?"

Kevin answered, "Sure, but I didn't think it was anything."

"Thanks."

The two men cruised the base. They liked one another but hadn't known each other long enough to be friends. Two things impressed themselves on Liberty's mind that night. The first was when Kevin, without provocation and in reference to his partner's leaving for the States, said, "When I get out, I'm moving to where there ain't any Greeks." He was surprised by Kevin's bitterness.

The other thing was of much more importance except that Liberty hadn't realized it at the time. Kevin had said, "I saw Whittle taking some televisions out of his car and putting them into a Greek's car in the parking lot right across from the base. I hate that bastard!"

Liberty knew that Whittle was in the black market on a small scale. Briefly, he wondered if Kevin was going to rat on Whittle and thought it unlikely; he didn't seem to be the kind of man to do that. Despite this, he decided to warn his friend that he was becoming too careless.

When he was relieved that morning, Liberty was too full of emotion to think of Whittle. It was his last night of work and he would never see most of these men ever again. In less than two weeks, he would be on a college campus and he was sad and a little frightened to leave this land that had become his home. He practically ran off base to catch some sleep before he started out-processing.

The two-hour ride from the civilian airport to Dover Air Force Base in Delaware took a couple of hours. Most of his out-processing had already been done in Greece, but the final touches, including the DD-214 discharge papers, would happen here. He and three other men had been picked up at the airport and taken to a van driven by a civilian. It was late in the evening and Liberty felt himself to be very much a stranger. For the last three years, America had seemed so far away and today, on U.S. soil, it still seemed that way.

Two things struck him as being very odd. The first was that everything, the houses, the stores, and the cars, especially the cars, all seemed so new. Nothing seemed to be older than ten years while in Greece, nothing seemed to be under thirty years old. Here everything was clean and flashy and fast. In Greece, everything was dusty and slow, or so it seemed. It seemed as though, since it was Friday night, that the air around the fast-moving cars was vibrant, almost electric. Everyone seemed to be excited.

The other odd thing was that when the van started taking secondary roads to the base, it made full stops at all railroad crossings. Liberty didn't know whether such caution was stupid, foolish, or wise. Someone decided that it was a wise thing to do, but Liberty was not used to anything remotely resembling caution.

Once on base, the four men were each assigned a room. Someone had thoughtfully made the bed so that Liberty only had to lie down and go to sleep. The sergeant who assigned them their rooms told them to show up at Personnel at 0800 hours. The mess hall would be open if they wanted breakfast.

Liberty's bunk was below the only window in the room. As he lay in the bunk, he stared out into the blackness. He literally could see nothing. His whole life seemed to be nothing. He really had nowhere to go although he had been accepted to Rhode Island College and knew that in two weeks he'd be living in a dorm and taking classes with people just out of high school.

He slept soundly. At 0700 his travel alarm woke him up. He didn't intend to go to the mess hall for breakfast since he didn't know where it was and the sooner he was done out-processing, the better.

At Personnel he met a staff sergeant who had volunteered to come into work on a Saturday to discharge the four men. Otherwise, they would all have to wait until Monday. Why would the staff sergeant care if they had to wait a couple of extra days before going home? But he did.

While the staff sergeant was giving them a plethora of forms to fill out, Liberty's three companions were more than overjoyed to be in America. They were ecstatic. They then told him how they had been stranded in Turkey for almost a year. All three had been caught with pot by the Turks, but had managed to make it to Incirlik Air Base before the Turkish police could haul them to jail. Day and night the Turks watched the base, hoping that the airmen would go off it, if only for a moment, so they could be arrested. For a year, the airmen lived on base and never stepped foot outside the chain link fence surrounding it. Finally, they were smuggled out in U.S. mail bags. The three men laughed in a jolly way and seemed both pleased and proud of their accomplishment. Along with Liberty, they would be getting an honorable discharge.

Liberty knew what the Greeks and Turks thought about drugs. He knew of the severe punishments, up to twenty-five years in fever-infested, filthy jails, that came with the possession of a single joint. Looking at his jolly companions, he thought, *what fools!*

It was still early morning when the men were finished with their out-processing. Each had his DD-214 to prove that he was a good citizen and a veteran. Liberty took his duffle bag, strapped it about his shoulders, and took another base van to another, closer, civilian airport. He took the first flight to Warwick, Rhode Island, and caught a taxi to his final destination – home.

Six years later, Claudius Boatman was walking from his apartment in New York City to The New School for Social Research where he took graduate courses in philosophy. As he walked along buildings that looked like rotted teeth, he became aware of a Black man walking beside him, matching his stride. Immediately, he felt the threat. As he turned to face the man, he realized that he knew him, a face without a name.

The Black man said, "Remember me?"

"Yes, I do. From Greece, but I don't remember your name."

"Bob Body."

"How could I forget? Sorry. Mine's Claudius Boatman."

"I know."

Neither man was interested in the other. Neither wanted to know what the other man was doing, but they had one thing in common. Bob said, "A lot happened after you left. Frick and Whittle were court-martialed for black marketeering. Frick got a reprimand and Whittle was dishonorably discharged."

"That's too bad."

"Do you remember that guy who turned everybody in once he got caught dealing drugs?"

"Donovan?"

"Yeah, supposedly he was murdered once he got stateside. Supposedly Siebold did it or at least Siebold was seen in the area when he was killed. It was a car bomb."

"That sounds like an urban legend to me."

"I find it hard to believe, too. That kind of crap happens only in the movies. It's a miracle *you* never killed anyone, or did you?"

"It *is* a miracle and, no, I never killed anyone. Do you know that no matter how many times I'd turn my back on people, waiting to get jumped, no one ever took the bait? I don't get it."

"What's there to get? What man in his right mind would ever attack a sociopath or a psychopath or whatever you were, and, let's face it, one look at you and they knew you were bouncing off the walls."

"I guess."

As the two men came to a corner, Bob said, pointing to the left, "I'm going that way."

"I'm going straight."

As Bob turned away, he said, "Have a good life."

"You, too."

Claudius wondered if Kevin had turned Whittle in and he wished he had warned the sergeant. But that was all in the past and, for Claudius, the 7206 Support Group, Athens, Greece, no longer existed. He would miss them.

ABOUT THE AUTHOR

Tom Doughty graduated from high school in 1968 during the Vietnam War. Two years later he was a security policeman in the U.S. Air Force and served for six months at the North American Aerospace Defense Command (NORAD) in Colorado and the three following years at Athenai Airbase in Athens, Greece. After his discharge, he earned a bachelor's degree and a master's degree in English. During the first Gulf War, he enlisted into the Army National Guard, then transferred to the Air Guard for a total of 19 years as a Guard member to achieve the rank of Master Sergeant. He is currently retired and living with his wife of 35 years and his two wonderful daughters.